Satan's Fury MC

by

L. Wilder

Satan's Fury MC
Copyright 2017 L. Wilder
All rights reserved.

L. Wilder

www.lwilderbooks.com

Cover Model: Dylan Horsch
www.facebook.com/DylanHorsch

Photographer: Wander Book Club
www.wanderbookclub.com

Cover Design: Mayhem Cover Creations
www.facebook.com/MayhemCoverCreations

Editor / Formatter: Daryl Banner
www.facebook.com/darylbannerwriter
www.darylbanner.com

Teasers & Banners: Gel Ytayz at Tempting Illustrations

Personal Assistant: Amanda Faulkner
www.facebook.com/amanda.faulkner.1023

– In The Series –

Catch up with the entire Satan's Fury MC Series today!
All books are FREE with Kindle Unlimited!

Summer Storm (Satan's Fury MC Novella)

Maverick (Satan's Fury MC #1)

Stitch (Satan's Fury MC #2)

Cotton (Satan's Fury MC #3)

Clutch (Satan's Fury MC #4)

Smokey (Satan's Fury MC #5)

You can also check out the Devil Chasers in the new
Boxed Set!!

Dedication

To My Grandmother:

Thank you for always believing in me.

Table of Contents

Satan's Fury MC

Book 6

Prologue
Mike

"Well, look who we have here," Baker snickered as he sauntered into the room with several of his hood rats following close behind.

My eyes skirted over to him and my chest tightened into a knot as I watched them file into the room. Baker was a big brute, weighing around two sixty with muscles protruding through his orange jumpsuit, while I was a tall, puny fucker who weighed a buck fifty with boots on. I was scared out of my damned mind, and rightly so. I knew what was coming. I'd seen it too many times to count, and I knew there was nothing I could do to stop it. I was stuck. I hated that feeling of helplessness and had always done my best to avoid it at all costs. I thought if I just kept my mouth shut and avoided all the roughnecks, I would be able to stay off their radar. But keeping off the grid in a place like this was damn near impossible. The GH Juvenile Detention Center was no place for a kid like me, but like a line of dominoes, the choices I'd made had landed me behind bars. I thought I was slick, that I wouldn't get caught, but I was wrong. I was wrong about a lot of damned things, and it's one of the reasons I'd found myself in the boys' bathroom surrounded by a pack of hungry wolves.

"You think you're so fucking smart. You walk around here acting like you're better than everyone else, but you ain't shit!" Baker snarled.

Baker was a grade A asshole, and over his stint in juvie, he'd acquired quite a following. He and his cronies had a thing for fucking with anyone who was smaller or weaker than them, and with my scrawny ass, there was no doubt I was an easy target. He stood there glaring at me like some rabid dog, and I knew he had his mind set on annihilating me. I felt the walls closing in as I looked towards the door. My fight or flight instincts kicked in and I felt an overwhelming urge to get the hell out of there, but a couple of his goons were guarding the exit. There was no way out. Knowing I was cornered, Baker's lips curled into a cold, heartless smile. There was no honor in fights like this. No code. It was simply the survival of the fittest, and I was damned from the start.

I swallowed hard and muttered, "I don't want any trouble, Baker."

"Nobody asked you what you wanted, you fucking pussy," he barked as he slammed his fist into my gut. Before I had a chance to defend myself, he reared back and punched me again right in the damn nose. Tears filled my eyes as I stumbled and fell flat on my face. As soon as my limp body hit the floor, he started kicking me in my side and abdomen causing me to curl into a protective ball. Bile burned at the back of my throat and the stench of piss and body odor only made it harder to resist the urge to puke. Laughter filled the room as I tried unsuccessfully to lift myself off the ground. Wobbling like a ninety-year-old heart patient, I didn't get very far. My arms felt like lead weights and my legs were quivering from the pain, making it impossible to move.

"We gotta get the hell out of here. The guards are gonna come looking for us," one of the guys urged. Their sneakers squeaked against the cold, concrete floor as they paced nervously back and forth. They were getting anxious, and I prayed they'd convince him to leave.

"We've got time. They're dealing with Duncan," Baker snickered. "Besides, I'm not done with our little computer freak just yet."

Baker was right. Duncan, one of the more emotionally disturbed kids in our hall, had one of his meltdowns, and it would take them all to get him settled back down. They wouldn't be coming anytime soon, and my hopes of someone coming to my rescue were completely squashed.

"I'm done with this bullshit. He'd not worth the trouble," one of them grumbled as he walked out the door.

"I knew you were a pussy, but I thought you'd at least put up a fight." Baker gave me a shove with his foot and snickered. "Come on, douchebag. Get up."

I was down, but I wasn't completely out. His words

were like a spark, fueling the fire that burned deep inside me. I couldn't give up—not just yet. Bruised and winded, I mustered the strength to stand. Anger exploded within me as I shouted, "Fuck you, Baker."

I held my breath as I took a swing at him. Satisfaction shot through me when the contact made his head jerk back. I'd thought I'd gotten him good, but my sense of pride was short-lived as his balled fist collided with my cheekbone. Everything went blurry, and I lost my footing. In a matter of seconds, my face was planted back on the bathroom floor. It was pathetic.

Baker lowered himself down on top of me and brought his mouth over to my ear. He whispered in a raw, guttural voice, "Is that all you got, pussy?"

I struggled against him, shooting my left leg out as I tried to get him off me, but I just wasn't strong enough. His hands moved up to my neck, wrapping tightly around my throat as he spat, "Where ya trying to run off to, freak-show? I'm not done with you yet."

I felt him reach into his back pocket and froze when I heard one of the guys yelp, "Don't Baker. You taking this too far."

"Shut your fucking mouth, Smith. I'll decide how far this thing goes!"

I twisted and turned, trying my best to buck him off me, but he just pressed his weight down on my body, pinning me against the concrete floor.

"Don't," I pleaded. "Just let me go. I'll keep my mouth shut. Just let me go."

Big

"Oh, you'll keep your fucking mouth shut or I'll finish what I started."

A burning sensation rushed through my side as the blade sank deep into my lower abdomen. He twisted the knife in his hand while sinking it deeper and deeper into my flesh. I tried to hold back my cries, but the pain was too much. My screams echoed through the concrete walls, causing everyone to scatter like flies. I lay there feeling my life drain from my body, and it was in that moment that I decided I'd never be the victim again.

It took some work, but I kept the promise I'd made to myself that day. As soon as I got out of the infirmary, the guards put me in solitary for the rest of my stint in juvie. Since they had no clue who had gotten to me, the counselors said I would be safer there. Once my wounds had healed and I was back on my feet, I started working out – hours upon hours of push-ups and squats, along with any other damned exercise I could come up with in the confines of that little room. One of the guards noticed what I was up to, and thinking it would be good for me, he gave me access to the weight room when no one else was around. When I walked out of that detention center six months later, I'd gained the muscle I was after, and that's when I realized Baker actually had done me a favor.

It was only two years later when I found myself behind bars for the second time, only now, I was six-foot-four and two hundred and seventy pounds of muscle. I was stronger, mentally and physically, but that didn't mean the guys didn't try to fuck with me. It was no secret why I'd been locked up. I was different, knew things these men didn't understand, and they sure as fuck didn't like it. Computer hacking wasn't exactly a crime a typical thug understood, and the unknown brought a level of fear, a fear I learned to use to my advantage.

It was after dinner, and I was heading back to my cell when my attention was drawn over to the cell next to mine. It was Jacob's cell, the only person I ever really talked to in this joint. He was a decent guy – for a gun trafficking murderer – and talking to him helped pass the time. When I stepped inside the cell, Tank, one of the Hispanic gang members, had Jacob pinned to the wall with his fingers wound tightly around his neck. I knew I didn't need any more violations added to my record, but there was no way I was going to let him fuck with Jacob.

I stepped closer and growled, "Drop him."

Without loosening his gripe, Tank turned to me and spat, "This isn't your fight, asshole. Get the fuck out."

"Not leaving until you let him go." I looked over at Jacob, and though he'd never admit it, he was struggling. The veins in his neck were bulging, and even through all his tattoos, I could see that his face was turning blue. "Now, Tank."

His eyes glaring with anger, he snarled, "You just signed your own death sentence, motherfucker."

I took a step forward and slammed my fist into his

ribcage over and over until he dropped his hold on Jacob. I reared back my closed fist and slammed it into the side of his jaw, causing him to lose his balance and fall back against the cot. He shook his head, trying to shake off the confusion, but I didn't give him that chance. I grabbed him by the neck, squeezing him tightly around the throat like he'd done Jacob and said, "This is over, Tank. You wanna know why it's over?" When he didn't answer, I continued. "Because if you even look in his direction, I will *end you*. I'll beat the goddamned life right out of you, make you beg for me to just let you die, and then I'll fuck with you in ways you can't even begin to imagine. And not just you, Santiago Rodrigues from Fallbrook, California. I will fuck with everyone you have ever known or cared about, and you'll never even see me coming. Got me?"

He nodded, and as soon as I released him, he scurried out of the cell like a wounded rat.

I turned to Jacob. "You wanna tell me what that was all about?"

"Nope."

"Didn't think so."

As I started back towards my cell, Jacob called, "Yo, Big."

"Yeah?"

"You're supposed to be getting out next week, right?"

"That's what they've been telling me."

"You headed back home when you're released?"

My mind involuntarily drifted back to my father. He'd always held on to the hope that I'd give up computers and hacking, that I'd find a new focus. I tried, but nothing could surpass the thrill I got from sitting behind that screen. I got a high from pushing limits, ignoring boundaries, and succeeding at things no one else could. It was my obsession, and I was getting better with every click of my keyboard. Unfortunately, I wasn't the only one getting better. The world of technology was changing and becoming harder to crack, and one mistake would cost more than it ever had before. My father knew the risks and warned me about them time and time again. After I was arrested the second time, he'd made it clear that I wasn't welcome back home. He was done trying to make me different.

"Nope. Nothing there for me."

"You should head up to Clallam County. Got some friends there you should meet. I think they could use a guy like you."

"A guy like me?"

"You and your particular skill set might come in handy, but it will be up to you to convince them of that."

"And why would I do that?"

"You're just gonna have to trust me on this one. Go out on Highway 61 and turn left at the fork on Millbrook Road. Drive about five miles and you'll see an old warehouse off on the left. Pull up to the gate and ask for Cotton. Tell him Nitro sent ya."

Chapter 1

"Hey, Big." Wren smiled as she peaked her head inside my room. "Would you mind helping me with something?"

"Sure." Wren is Stitch's old lady. Some would say they are an unlikely match, but I disagree. Wren had a way about her. Without even trying, she could break through the walls we put up and see the good that lies behind them. Stitch is one of the toughest guys I know. He's downright intimidating at times, but he's always been willing to do anything to protect the people he cares about. Wren saw past his rough exterior and found the heart hidden beneath. She and Wyatt, and now Mia, have been the best thing that ever happened to him. "Whatcha got?"

"It's Wyatt. He's trying to hook up his new game system in the family room, and he isn't having much luck. I don't have a clue how to do it, so…"

I stood up from my computer and walked over to her. Mia was sleeping soundly in the crook of her arm. She was all dolled up in one of those soft pink outfits with a little pink beanie on her head. Hard to believe Stitch's kid could be so damn cute.

"I'll get him fixed up."

Relief washed over her as she said, "I'd appreciate

it. He wants to have it ready when Dusty gets here, otherwise I wouldn't have bothered you."

"Not a problem."

I followed her out into the hall and down to the family room. When we walked in, Wyatt had cords and remotes scattered all over the room. From the scowl on his face, I could see that he was getting frustrated. He bit at his bottom lip as he tried to force the HDMI cable into the side of the TV, and I had to swallow my smile. I'd always seen a lot of myself in Wyatt, knowing his brain worked differently than most, and I understood his aggravation. Like me, he wanted to get it right the first time. "Need a hand?"

"I can get it," he grumbled.

"I'm sure you can." I walked over to the coffee table and picked up the box with his new PlayStation and said, "I've been wanting to check this out for weeks. Stitch get this for you?"

Without looking in my direction, he answered, "Yes, sir. Made all A's on my report card."

Wren smiled with pride as she said, "He was the only one in his class."

"All A's. That's pretty impressive, dude."

He let out a sigh as he turned towards me and offered me the cable. "Can you do this? I can't get it to go in."

I took it from his hand and slid it into the correct slot. Together, we took the remaining parts out of the box and in a matter of minutes, we had it all up and running. Wyatt and I settled ourselves on the large, L-shaped sofa and started playing *Call of Duty*. We were both lost in the game when Wren asked, "Hey, Big. Have you heard from Tristen?"

"Not since she left." She'd gone to Mexico with one of her girlfriends for a couple of days. We all understood why she needed a break from the club. She had a thing for Smokey, and while we all knew he didn't feel the same – including Tristen – it hurt her when he fell for MJ.

"I thought they were supposed to be back yesterday."

"You know how things go in Mexico. Maybe they just decided to stay a little longer."

"Maybe," she answered in a low, concerned voice.

"I'm sure she's fine. If we haven't heard from her by tomorrow, I'll check on her," I offered.

"You're right. I'm sure she's okay."

"There a reason why you needed her?"

She looked down at Mia cradled in her arms. "I just wanted to see if she could watch Wyatt while we went for the baby's checkup."

"I can keep an eye on him."

"Are you sure?"

I gave Wyatt a little nudge with my elbow as I said, "Gotta figure out how to beat him at this game. Figure it's gonna take a while."

"That would be great. I'll be back in a couple of hours, and if you need anything, just call."

"Take your time," I told her as I tried to return my focus to the game. I was surprised to see that Wyatt was already two kills ahead of me. "Damn, dude. You're good at this."

Never losing his focus, he fired off several rounds against the enemy. "You can catch up. Make your advance, stay covered, and change your weapon. That one is for girls."

"Is that right?"

"I thought you knew that kind of stuff," Wyatt taunted.

"Guess I still have a lot to learn." I laughed as I switched to my secondary and tried to catch up to him. We hadn't been playing long when Dusty came in. Needless to say, I lost my spot on the sofa and the boys quickly forgot I was even in the room. I sat back in the recliner and smiled as I watched them play. They were good together—two little amigos that had found a friendship that would last them a lifetime.

Once Wren returned from the baby's appointment, I went back to my room and got to work. Over the past few months, I'd been busy. The demand for weapons was continuing to increase, and in order to keep up, the club had to make some changes. We'd done well with our shipments in the past, managed to stay under that ATF's radar, but with the increase in deliveries, it would be harder to stay that way. It was time for us to start buying the parts separately, which would make it easier to ship them without detection and leave the full assembly to be done once they reached Mexico. It was up to me to check out Nitro's new contacts and make sure they didn't have any skeletons lurking in the closet. He had his own people for this sort of thing, but he wanted me to be there to double check their findings. Nitro wasn't a man who took chances, and that's why Cotton used him. Over the years, we'd established an understanding. We all knew in our line of work there were high expectations and the failure to bring results would bring consequences that threatened to pull us under.

I'd gone through the first guy with no real red flags, but the second was a different story. I knew right away something was up with him. I picked up my phone and called Nitro. As soon as he answered, I blurted, "You've gotta be fucking kidding me?"

"About?"

"Claybrooks."

"You mean the cop?"

"Damn. You had me worried there for a minute." We'd had our run-ins with cops in the past, each one thinking he'd found his way inside, but none had ever made it very far. It was evident that Claybrooks was working an undercover op, and it wasn't like Nitro not to smell him from a mile away.

"Yeah, I thought you could have a little fun with him," Nitro snickered. "Give him something to occupy his time for a while."

"You want me to bury him?"

"Make an impression."

"You got it."

As soon as I hung up the phone, I started working on Mr. Jonathan Claybrooks, aka Detective David Keen. I sent a phishing email requesting to run an update on his computer's security, and within the hour, he'd responded with everything I needed—his password, home address, pin, email addresses, and his social. Once I had that information, there was nothing I couldn't do. I started with his email contacts, sending evidence of misconduct to his commanding officer and the mayor. It would only be a matter of time before he'd lose his job, but that wasn't enough. Before I closed out his email, I sent a malicious virus to everyone on his contact list, making sure they all knew he was behind the destruction of their own personal security. I reported his car stolen, triggering his vehicle's security system to send a remote signal that blocked the engine from starting. Then, I moved on to his bank accounts, completely clearing his checking and savings accounts. After I had his cell phone and utilities shut off, I attacked his social media, slamming his Facebook, Twitter, and Instagram pages with goat porn and golden showers, along with photoshopped pics of him wearing KKK t-shirts and hats – just enough to leave a lasting impression on everyone who knew him. Finally, just for fun, I changed all his passwords and added a required updated pin to each, making it frustrating as hell for him to regain access to any of his accounts.

Big

I leaned back in my chair and stared at the computer screen with a sense of satisfaction, knowing that I'd just yanked the rug out from underneath Keen. Sure, there was the possibility that over time he could convince people that he'd been hacked and get his life back, but the damage had been done. That element of doubt would always be there, leaving a lasting scar on his reputation. Every time he picked up his phone, each time he logged into his computer or used his debit card, he would remember this day and the panic he'd felt. After today, Keen and all those detective pricks would think twice before they fucked with Nitro again. I was just about to add his name to the possible American terrorist list, FAA No-Fly, and DHS Homegrown, when there was a knock on my door.

"Yo, Big Mike." Q' stuck his head inside. "You heard anything about Tristen? Some chick keeps calling the bar. Says she's been trying to call her cell but can't get her to answer."

Hearing her name for the second time that day gave me an uneasy feeling. Tristen had been with the club for just over a year. At first, she was just one of the hang arounds, looking for a good time with no real connection to any of the guys, but over time, she started to make herself useful. She did what she could to help around the bar and in the kitchen, and it didn't go unnoticed. When Cotton found out she was a runaway, he hired her and set her up in one of the rooms at the club. She seemed happy, like the club was her home. It wasn't like her not to answer the phone, or let us know that her plans had changed. "Has anyone been able to reach her?"

"Not that I know of. You mind talking to this chick and see if you can get her to chill the fuck out?"

"Yeah. I'll see what I can do," I told him as I stood up and followed him back to the bar. When I picked up the phone and put it up to my ear, the line was dead. "She hung up."

"Guess it wasn't that important after all."

"Did she say who she was?"

"Nope. Just that she was looking for Tristen."

"Yeah. I guess I better see if I can figure out what's going on with her."

"Bet she found her some guy down there in Mexico. Liable to just move down there or something. Not like there's anything holding her here."

"She's got us."

"But not in the way she wants. Girls like her will always want more… and honestly, she deserves it. She's a good kid. Maybe she finally found what she's been looking for."

"Stranger things have happened, but I'll do some checking just to be sure."

"Let me know what you find out."

I went back to my room, and as soon as I logged into my computer, there was a glitch in the screen. To anyone else, it would look like nothing – just a flicker – but I knew all too well what it meant. Someone had synced a rat to one of our servers using a remote access tool. They were slick, but not slick enough to get past me. I picked up my burner and made a call to Cotton.

When he answered, I said, "We've got trouble. You better come check this out."

"I'm on my way."

As soon as I hung up, I started a counter attack. They'd only managed to crack the outer layer of my security system, so I still had time to stop them before they got into our main database. I started with an intrusion inspection, so I could find exactly where they were located. To do that, I would need their IP address. They were using an encrypted network, so all the traffic was routed through relays, making it difficult to locate them.

I was still working to find the exact address when Cotton came charging through the door. "What's wrong?"

Without looking away from my computer, I answered, "We got ourselves a hacker."

"Damn it."

Cotton leaned over me, watching as I typed away on my keyboard. Even with him breathing down the back of my neck, I managed to get the IP address. I was surprised to see it was coming from an apartment building only a few miles away. "Got him." I wrote down the address and handed it to Cotton. "We need to get someone over there, now."

"I'll send Stitch and Maverick."

"Make sure they get *everything*. Computers. Phones. Anything this guy might be using. We need to know what the hell he's after."

Cotton made the call, and once he had everything sorted, he turned back to me. "Got any idea who this guy might be?"

"No idea. I'm going to do what I can to slow him down, but I gotta tell you... whoever this is, he knows what he's doing. In a matter of minutes, he breeched my firewall."

"You gonna be able to hold him off?"

"I've got this covered. Just let me know when they get back to the club with this guy."

"You got it."

Once he was gone, I considered launching a virus, but decided to hold off. I wanted to have access to everything they had on their computer, knowing I may need it later. I bombarded their server with garbage files, making it impossible for them to get any further into our system. Going up against another hacker is like trying to solve a Rubik's Cube that keeps changing just as you get the first pattern in place. I was making headway when it became apparent that my assailant was no longer there. It wasn't long before I got word from Stitch that they'd gotten our guy and were heading back to the clubhouse. I knew where they'd be taking him. When there were questions to be answered, questions that some guys weren't so willing to answer, Stitch brought them to his playroom. It was a place where he didn't have any problems getting answers.

Knowing they'd be back any minute, I grabbed my laptop and started towards the back of the clubhouse. When I walked into the room, Maverick gave me a strange look—a look I might expect if I was about to be the brunt of some joke, not the kind I'd expect after they'd just apprehended the guy who'd just tried to hack into our database. I stopped dead in my tracks and asked, "What?"

He smirked as he motioned to a chair centered in the back of the room. "We got the big, badass hacker for ya."

His sarcasm didn't go unnoticed as I looked over to see who they'd bound to the chair. I'll admit I had my own thoughts about who our hacker could've been – maybe an old enemy that resurfaced to take his revenge, or a member of an MC that was set on taking down our club. There'd been a hundred different ideas that crossed my mind over the past hour, but never once did I ever imagine that it could've been the person sitting in that chair. I glanced back over at Maverick and growled, "You've got to be fucking kidding me."

"Nope."

I looked back over at the beautiful blonde with emerald green eyes as I ran my hand through my hair. "Well, I'll be damned."

Chapter 2
Josie

"You got a name?" the older guy asked, but I didn't answer. On any other day, I might be inclined to talk to the handsome biker, but today, under these circumstances, there was no way in hell I was gonna talk. I couldn't. There was too much at risk. No matter what happened, I had to keep my mouth shut and bide my time. I couldn't show any sign of weakness or everything I'd been fighting for would come crashing down around me – or worse, they'd kill me.

He took a step closer and knelt in front of me, glaring in a way that made my skin crawl. I twisted and tugged against the restraints around my wrists, hoping that I might be able to slip my hands free, but it was pointless; they were on too tight. "Who do you work for? Why were you trying to hack into my club?"

I didn't answer. I just sat there silently staring back at him, and it was clear from the expression on his face that it was just making him even angrier. He stood up, slowly walked behind me, and then I felt a blade rake against my skin. My hands were released, giving me a false sense of relief, but only momentarily. He reached out and grabbed my arm, jerking me up on my feet. He tugged me towards the center of the room, and panic started to set in when I noticed a chain hanging from the ceiling. I tried to break free, but there was no getting away from him. Just as I feared he would, he cuffed my hands to the chain, making it impossible to get free.

"Do you know where you are?" he asked as he motioned over to the guy with the long, black beard and coal-black eyes. "This is *his* room. Any idea what he uses it for?"

The looks of the man were enough to scare me, but my fear hit an all-time high when I started to look around the room. There was a metal gurney in the back, and strange machines and contraptions hanging on the walls. It took me several seconds to comprehend all the different things I was seeing, but when I noticed the assortment of knives and chemicals on the long counter, I quickly realized exactly what the room was used for. My stomach turned and bile rose to my throat as my imagination began to run wild. I couldn't stop thinking of all the things he might do in this room—and what he might do to me.

"Now, I am going to ask you again. *Who are you and what do you want with my club*?" he snarled.

The answer was sitting there on the tip of my tongue, begging to be released, but I clamped my lips shut and remained silent. I had to hold it together. When I didn't answer, his eyebrows furrowed and one of the veins in his neck started to bulge out, making me feel a slight sense of satisfaction that I was getting to him. I waited patiently for him to make his next move. The last of his restraint went flying out the window when he reached up and took a hold of my face. His fingers dug into my cheeks as he forced me to look at him.

"You think you can come after my club and get away with it? You've gotta be out of your fucking mind. No one fucks with my club. *No one*." He released his hold on me and turned his attention to one of the guys in the back of the room. "Big, grab her laptop. See if you can find out what the hell she's been up to." Then, he looked back at me. "Don't reckon you're gonna give me the password for that damned thing?"

I knew their guy was good, probably one of the best I'd ever encountered. Knowing it would only be a matter of time before he'd hack into my computer, I had wiped it clean – at least as much as I could in the short amount of time I'd had. It would take him some time, but he'd find what he was looking for. I knew I could just give him the password, make it easier on myself, but I'd never been one to do things the easy way. Besides, I needed him distracted. The longer he was working on my computer, the less he'd be on his.

"Doesn't matter. I can get in," the big guy assured him as he reached for my laptop. When he picked it up, a brown liquid came trickling out of the side. He looked over to me with a questioning look, and I had to suppress my smile as I remembered that I'd poured my soda over it just as they'd broken into the apartment. He rolled his eyes, then gave it a hard shake, forcing more of the cola out of the keyboard as he started for the door. "You know where I'll be."

Big

As soon as he was gone, the older man walked over to the two remaining men in the back of the room. The guy with the short, dark hair and green eyes never took his eyes off me as they discussed their next move. They talked for several minutes, and then without warning, they started to file out of the room. Just before the door closed behind them, the lights turned off, and a blanket of darkness fell over me. While I could no longer see what was hidden in the pitch-black, I knew what was there. I tried my best not to think about it. I tried to conjure up a story in my head or an old memory that could help me forget that I was hanging from a chain awaiting my demise, but every thought led back to him—the man with the long beard and dark, threatening eyes. I just had to hold on a bit longer, but each second seemed like an eternity as I hung there suspended in the darkness. It felt like I'd been there for hours when the room started to feel colder, much colder, to the point that the tips of my fingers and nose became numb. I don't know how they'd done it, but they managed to drop the temperature dramatically, making me feel like a piece of meat hanging in a freezer. The cold air felt heavy against my skin as it stole the warmth from my body. My teeth started to chatter and the shivers set in, making it difficult to concentrate. I'd almost forgotten where I was until the lights flickered on and I caught sight of him standing in the door way.

"Gets pretty damn cold in here, doesn't it? Place can drop forty degrees in less than half an hour."

My heart started to beat wildly against my chest as he started walking towards me.

Paying no mind to the freezing temperature, he slowly removed his leather jacket and placed it on the back of a chair. As he approached me, his eyes locked on mine. "You're no different than anybody else. Everybody's got secrets." His voice was low and full of warning as he spoke. "It's my job to find out what those secrets are, and you should know... I'm good at my job."

He took a black and white bandana from his back pocket and used it to cover my eyes, blindfolding me as he continued to talk. "How far this thing goes is up to you." I felt the cold air bite against my stomach as he began to unbutton my shirt, stopping just below the edge of my bra so only my lower abdomen was exposed. "How much this hurts is up to you."

I had no idea what he meant, but I was about to find out. Before I had a chance to brace myself, there was a crackling sound followed by a strong, painful tingling against my stomach. Every muscle in my body drew tense as an electric current flowed through me. It was like a thousand tiny pins and needles stabbed my fingers, toes, arms, and throughout my entire body. A sour taste filled my mouth, and the tightness in my chest made it difficult to breathe. I had no idea how long it lasted, but it felt like a lifetime. I was just about to pass out when the shock suddenly stopped and my body fell limp against the restraints.

"Hurts like a motherfucker, don't it?" he mocked.

In that moment, doubts started to bombard my mind. There was no way I was getting out of this. There was no knight in shining armor coming to my rescue, and my reasons for keeping silent suddenly didn't seem to matter. Either I told him what I was doing there, or he was going to kill me. End of story. I was still considering my next move when I felt the tingling sensation again. I clenched my jaw and held my breath, bracing myself for the next shock. This time, he held the current against my flesh longer, making the sensation much more intense and much harder to maintain consciousness. My body jolted and a fog fell over me, making me feel like one of those cartoons with stars and bright lights whirling above their head. Then, everything went black.

I don't know how long I'd been out, but it must've been too long for Mr. Terror because he tossed a bucket of cold water over my head. "Shit!"

"Well, lookie there. She *can* speak." I heard his boots squeak against the wet concrete as he walked back over to me. "Did you have a nice nap?"

"It was lovely. Thanks for asking, dickhole."

He reached behind me and grabbed a hold of my hair. "You got anything you want to tell me?"

"Eat shit and die," I grumbled.

"I'm gonna do you a favor and give you a heads-up here. Now that you are wet, this is gonna hurt a hell of a lot more." He released his grip on my hair, then zapped me once again. Numbing pain shot through me, and my body convulsed with the shock. He was right; it hurt twice as much, and I passed out within the first few seconds.

When I finally regained consciousness, I was surprised to find that my blindfold had been removed. After a few seconds of letting my eyes adjust to the light, I looked up and found my assailant sitting on a stool smoking a cigarette. There was no sweat on his brow, his hair was still perfectly combed back, and his shirt wasn't the least bit wrinkled. He seemed completely unaffected by the fact that he'd been torturing me for hours while I was falling apart. Every muscle in my body ached and burned, my clothes were sopping wet, I was freezing cold, and I could barely keep my eyes open.

It was then that I started thinking their computer guy was better than I thought. I thought I could handle whatever he dished out for a few hours, but I was wrong. My plan was falling apart, and there was no sense in trying to hold out any longer. It was just too much. When I finally gathered the strength to speak, I mumbled, "I know what you did."

He took a tug off his cigarette and let the smoke billow around him as he glared at me. "Care to clarify that?"

"I know you killed her," I spat.

"Who?"

"You know damn well *who*!" I wanted to punch

him right in the face. The very idea that he would deny it repulsed me to no end. "I know you did it, and I know why! You were afraid she'd run her mouth... tell everyone about all the crazy shit you do here, so you killed her."

"You're stalling with this shit."

"You sit there acting like you are all tough and strong, but you are just a damned coward. Too afraid to admit what you did."

He took a step towards me, and I could feel the anger radiating from his body. "I don't take accusations like that lightly."

I should've taken that as a warning, but I let my anger deter my thinking. "I don't know what the hell she was thinking. She knew what kind of men you were. She should've known you would've come after her, but she trusted you... *all of you*."

"Enough of the bullshit. I'm tired of fucking around."

He stood up and tossed his cigarette to the floor, then he took the long, metal rod in his hand and started walking towards me. I knew he was about to shock me again, so I shouted, "Wait! You can't stop it without the code."

"What the hell are you talking about now?"

"If you kill me, you will never be able to stop it. You will lose everything." I knew he'd never admit what they'd done to my sister and in the end, I knew they were going to do the same thing to me, but I had to give it one last shot.

"I don't know shit about any fucking codes. You're just rambling a bunch of nonsense now. I'm done listening to your bullshit."

He was just about to hit me again when I heard a door open and a man shout, "Hold up, Stitch! Stop!"

Seconds later, he was behind me, releasing me from my restraints. Relief washed over me as my hands dropped to my side. I tried to take a step, but stumbled backwards. Just as I was about to hit the ground, I was lifted up into the air. Before I had a chance to resist, I was in his arms with my head resting comfortably on his shoulder. My mind was a blur. That's the only excuse I have for my actions. There was no other way to explain why I would be nestled close to his chest, feeling the warmth of his body against mine, when I should've been running for the door. Dammit! I was not following the plan.

The man he'd just called Stitch started walking towards us with a shocked expression on his face. "Am I missing something here?"

"Her name is Josie Carmichael."

"And?"

"She's Tristen's sister," he explained as he took a blanket from one of the cabinets and covered me, making my escape plan even more difficult. I wanted to protest, to tell him to fuck off and let me down, but I couldn't form the words. He continued to hold me protectively against his chest as he explained, "She's been looking for her, and she thinks we had something to do with her disappearance. She was looking in…" Before he could finish his sentence, the power went out. "Damn. It just keeps coming."

"What the fuck?" Stitch grumbled as he pulled a lighter out of his pocket and lit it.

"It's a blackout. She did a number on us. Slipped a virus in through the back door and compromised our entire hard drive. I did everything I could to slow it down, but…"

"Wait a minute. She did all that and knocked out our power?"

"I reckon she did. I've got to see how much of our system was wiped. We need to see if we can get the generators going before Cotton gets here."

As Stitch headed for the door, he said, "I'll take care of it. You just keep an eye on her."

Now that he was gone, I finally had my chance to get out of this place, to run, but unfortunately, I couldn't move. I needed a few more seconds to gather my strength. I was thinking about my next move when Big whispered in the darkness, "I don't guess you're gonna tell me how you did all this or why?"

"I had my reasons."

The lights flickered back on just as Stitch walked back into the room. "Well, I gotta say. I never saw that one coming."

"That goes for both of us."

Stitch shook his head as he walked back over to us.

"So, let me get this straight. All that shit you were saying about us killing someone... that was about *Tristen*? You really think we fucking killed her, so you hacked into our club, got yourself tortured, and wiped out our computer systems and power? Are you out of your fucking mind?"

There was something in his voice that made me start to question everything, and a world of doubt crashed around me. Before I could answer, Big whispered, "You've got it all wrong, Josie. We'd never hurt Tristen."

I looked up at him, saw the sincerity in his eyes, and for a moment, I actually believed him.

Chapter 3

Cotton charged into the room, but stopped cold when he found me holding Josie protectively in my arms. "What the fuck is going on?"

"Big Mike got into her computer."

"And?"

"She's not the threat we thought she was." Stitch looked over to Josie with his eyes filled with regret, and I could see that he was struggling. He'd let us know from the start that he didn't like the thought of hurting a woman. He assured us that he'd get the information we needed, but he made it clear there were boundaries he wasn't willing to cross. In the end, he did what had to be done, but knowing he'd tortured Josie unnecessarily was fucking with his head. "She's Tristen's sister."

While Stitch caught Cotton up on everything I'd found on her computer and the virus she'd used to crash our system, I turned my attention back to Josie. A spark of anger flickered in her eye as she pushed against my chest and demanded, "Put me *down*."

She winced with pain as I eased her down onto the counter. I had no idea what Stitch had done to her over the past four hours, but she looked like hell. Her body shivered and twitched as she gripped onto the edge of the counter. "Are you okay?"

"No. I'm not."

"Can I get you anything?"

"You can get me the hell out of here."

"That's not going to happen."

"Then how about an aspirin and a stiff drink?"

"Aspirin I can do." I walked over to the cabinet, grabbed the pain relievers and a bottle of water from the minifridge, then brought them back over to her. Her hand trembled as she reached for the water. "Stiff drink later."

"Make it two."

Her eyes skirted over to Cotton as she watched him walk over to us. After placing a timer down beside her, he pulled up a stool and sat down in front of her. "You've got ten minutes. Either you convince me that what you're saying is true or you go back on the hook."

"What exactly do you want from me?"

"I want the truth. I want to know how you got it in your head that we killed Tristen."

"I know what kind of men you are… the things you do in this so-called club."

"And what is that exactly?"

"I know that 1%er patch on your jacket means you aren't out there passing out bibles."

Cotton raised his eyebrow as he looked over at the timer. "The clock's ticking, kid. You're just digging a deeper hole."

"You got a young girl in your club, seeing things, hearing things, and you didn't like the fact that she'd had enough of all the bullshit and decided to move on. You were afraid she might run her mouth about things she'd seen and heard while she was here, so you made sure there was no way she could talk."

Cotton looked over at me. "Kid's got one hell of an imagination."

"When did she tell you she was leaving?" Stitch asked her.

"She was on her way to Mexico. Something was bugging her, but she wouldn't tell me what it was. I kept pushing, and that's when she said she'd decided to quit her job at the club."

I looked at Stitch. "Probably had something to do with Smokey."

"What about Smokey?"

Maverick answered, "She tried to be cool about it, but anyone could see she had a thing for him."

"So?" she pushed.

"So… he got himself an old lady."

"Of course, he did," she huffed. "She was never going to find the right guy in a motorcycle club. She was crazy to think she would. She thought of you as her family."

"We feel the same about her."

"That's not true and you know it. Tristen isn't your *family*. She's just some chick that would pick up your trash and put food on your table during the day, and a warm body to crawl in bed with at night. Do you even know about her past? The hell she's been through? Do you have any idea how hard she had it? She was just looking for a place where she could feel safe… where no one would hurt her again."

"We've been good to her," Cotton growled. "She's happy here."

"If she was so happy, why would she want to leave?" Josie sighed with frustration.

"That's something you'd have to ask her."

"I would if I knew where she was," Josie snapped.

"So, what makes you think she never made it to Mexico?" Cotton asked.

"I've called the hotel, and she never checked in. I've been calling her cell phone over and over, but she hasn't answered. Since the night at the airport, I haven't been able to reach her."

"Tell me about that phone call," Cotton ordered.

"I thought she was just tired. She mentioned she'd been feeling dizzy, so I told her to splash some water on her face. As soon as she stepped into the bathroom, the line went dead." Her eyes were filled with worry as she continued, "At first, I thought the call had just dropped or something. Thought it was just bad reception, but then I tried calling back and couldn't get her to answer. By the next morning, I knew something was wrong."

"And you've had no contact with her since that phone call?"

"No. And since you're denying that you had anything to do with her disappearance, have any of *you* talked to her?"

Big

The room fell silent. As far as we all knew, Tristen was living it up at the beach with one of her friends. None of us had reason to be concerned, so we left her alone. Cotton finally answered, "No."

"She's been gone for days, and none of you... her so-called family... even took the time to check up on her?"

"Tristen needed some time away. Besides, she's always had a mind of her own. As her sister, you should know that."

"She's young and naïve. I'll give her that, but this is extreme, even for her."

"It's late." Cotton stopped the timer and stood up. "Get her down to Tristen's room. Let her get a shower and a change of clothes. See what you can do to get our computers up and running again."

She shook her head frantically. "No. I want to go home."

"You should've thought about that before you hacked into my club and crashed our fucking hard drive," Cotton barked at her.

"It's an easy fix. I can give you the code, and you can have things back running in a matter of minutes. Just let me go home."

He handed her a sheet of paper. "Write it down."

Once she was done, she handed it back to him. "Now, just let me go home."

"That's not gonna happen. You're staying here until we get this thing sorted." He looked over at me.

"Big, keep an eye on her."

"Well, shit," Josie grumbled under her breath.

I walked over and helped Josie down from the counter. I took her arm, supporting her as she took her first steps, and we were just about to walk out of the room when Stitch stepped in our path. Her body tensed as he spoke. "You should've *said* something… anything to stop me from doing…"

"I was just biding my time, but it wouldn't have mattered anyway. You had a job to do."

"*No.* If you had just explained… told us what was going on…"

"It was my decision to make. Can't go back, so there's no point in trying to change things now."

She quietly held onto my arm as I led her into the clubhouse and down the hall to Tristen's room. When I opened the door, she released her hold on my arm and stepped inside. I watched as she walked around the room, studying all of her sister's pictures and knickknacks.

Tears filled her eyes as she turned to me. "Where could she be?"

Damn. She wasn't making it easy. Seeing her look so beautiful, but so broken, tore at me. I wanted to reach for her, pull her close to me and whisper promises in her ear, but reality kept me from moving towards her. Even though she thought she had reason, she'd done a real number on us. It was going to take me hours to get our computers back up, and we still had no concrete evidence that proved she was telling us the truth about who she was. Until I uncovered everything, every last detail about her and her past, Josie would remain a threat and had to be treated as such.

"I don't know, but I'll find her," I assured her. "It's what I do."

"I can help."

"No."

"At least let me get the power back on for you."

"And how are you going to do that?"

"Just need your phone for a minute." I reluctantly pulled it out of my back pocket and handed it over to her.

"You got something other than a burner?"

I grabbed my other cell and offered it to her. Seconds later, the lights flickered, letting us both know that everything was back up and running. She handed me back my phone as her lips curled into a prideful smile. I didn't bother asking how she'd done it. It was clear that she had her own connections to the utility department. "I can help with other stuff, too."

"Like Cotton said, it's late. You need to get some rest."

She crossed her arms and glared at me with determination. "It's not like I'm going to sleep... not when she could be out there needing me."

I took a step towards her and placed my hand on her shoulder. "You're no good to her like this. You're exhausted, beaten all to hell, and on top of all that, you're soaked to the bone. Now take a damn shower and get yourself some sleep."

I walked out and closed the door behind me. When I got back to my room, Cotton was sitting at my desk waiting for me. It had been a day from hell, and from the look on my president's face, I knew it was far from over. "We need to know if she's really Tristen's sister."

I walked over to my desk and reached for the file that had everything I'd found on her laptop. "I looked through their emails. They've been talking since the day Tristen moved in."

"Okay, but how do we know this is the same girl? The truth is, she could be anyone. She crashed our entire fucking system, Big. There's no doubt she's seen the same damn emails and could've used them to come up with that harebrained story of hers."

In my gut, I believed she was telling us the truth, but he had a point. We had no photographs of Tristen's sister, or any real means of proving Josie was actually who she said she was. "Agreed."

"You need to start digging. We have to know everything there is to know about Tristen and her sister."

"What exactly do we know about Tristen?"

"Not a lot. Her parents died in a car crash when she was sixteen. She ended up living with some aunt here in Washington. Tristen rebelled like teenagers do. Drinking. Partying. Got herself into some trouble. She hadn't been living with the aunt long when she ran away. Bounced around from place-to-place until I gave her a job here."

"And the sister?"

He ran his hand through his salt and pepper hair as he sighed. "There are two kinds of people in the world: those who thrive under adversity, and those who crumble beneath it. Tristen was lost, couldn't get her shit together after the death of her parents, while her sister went on to college and managed to make something of herself. It caused a rift between them, and I just assumed they never got back on track."

"Any idea where they grew up?"

"Massachusetts. Her dad was a professor at MIT."

"That explains her background with computers. I'll see what else I can find."

"While you're at it, check Tristen's flight. See how far she made it, and then call the hotel. See if she or her friend ever checked in. For all we know, all this mess with Josie is just some kind of diversion. We can't take any chances here. There is too much at stake."

"And what if she's telling the truth? What if Tristen really is missing?"

He started for the door as he said, "Then we find her and do whatever it takes to bring her home."

Chapter 4
Josie

I'd always wondered what kind of life Tristen had made for herself, and I was relieved to see that she was doing better than I'd imagined. When she told me she was living at an MC clubhouse, I'd pictured a place with concrete floors and old metal beds, but her room was nothing like that. It was actually nicer than my first apartment, with a pretty cherry bed set and small desk in the corner, and there was a flat screen TV mounted on the wall with brightly colored flowers on the dresser. It was full of charm and suited her perfectly. As pleased as I was that she had a nice room, being around her things made me miss her even more. There was a time when we were close, really close. We shared everything, even our bedroom, but things changed when Mom and Dad died.

Just a few weeks after our parents' funeral, I went off to college. The timing couldn't have been worse. She resented me for leaving her, feeling like I'd left her the same way our parents had, but I didn't have a choice. If I hadn't gone when I did, I would've lost my scholarship and any chance of ever getting my degree. I couldn't take that chance. I wanted to be able to help her, pick up the slack where my parents no longer could, and I couldn't do that working in a checkout line. She wouldn't talk to me for over a year, but then one day, out of the blue, she texted me. It wasn't much, but it was a start. From there, we started talking more and more. We were finally getting back on track, and I couldn't bear the thought of something happening to her.

My worries kept piling one on top of another, and I found myself crying once again. My mind was wrecked along with the rest of me. Big was right. I was physically and mentally drained, and I needed a hot shower.

After turning on the water, I tried to peel off my wet clothes, but they clung to my body, making it almost impossible to remove them. The fact that I was in agony didn't help matters. I was almost to the point of tears when I finally managed to get my jeans off and toss them on the floor. Just as I was about to step in the shower, I got a glimpse of myself in the mirror. I almost didn't recognize myself with the bruises and cuts on my wrists and the burns on my abdomen. Choosing to ignore my wounds, I hobbled into the shower and let the stream of warm water rush down my back. My muscles cried with relief while my burns stung like fire. I tried my best not to cry out in pain as I took the soap and carefully washed my wounds. Once I was done, I got out and put on one of Tristen's t-shirts and a pair of sweats. After I slipped on some oversized socks, I started for the bed. I was about to crawl in when there was a knock on the door. When I opened it, a man I'd never seen stood there.

"I'm Doc. Stitch sent me to see about you." Without my invitation, he stepped inside the room and placed his medical bag on the side table. "Need to check your wounds."

"Ummm. No. That's not necessary."

He reached for my hand. "No sense in being stubborn about it. We don't want these wounds getting infected." There was a kindness in his eyes that I wasn't expecting, so I didn't argue when he started bandaging my wrists. "Need to check your burns so I can see what we're dealing with."

The burns weren't bad, but I knew he was right. The last thing I needed was for them to get infected, so I raised the hem of my t-shirt just high enough for him to see them. "They aren't all that bad."

"You got lucky." He reached into his bag and took out a small jar of ointment. His hands were soft and gentle as he applied the medication and a loose bandage on my wounds. Once he was done, he reached in his bag again for a bottle of pills and then turned to me. "Put the cream on your burns twice a day, and the pain relievers as needed. Need to take a couple now. They will help you sleep tonight."

"Somehow, I doubt I'll be sleeping tonight."

"You might be surprised." He smiled as he started for the door.

There was something about him that reminded me of my grandfather. Maybe it was his lopsided smile or the fact that he smelled like old cigars and maple syrup. Whatever it was, he gave me a comforting feeling, a feeling that I could trust him. "Can I ask you a question?"

"You can ask. Doesn't mean I will answer."

"This guy, Cotton. He's the president of the club, right?"

"He is."

"Is he a good man?"

He looked me dead in the eye as he replied, "One of the best I know."

"Would you say these other guys – Stitch and Big – are they good men, too?"

"They are. I know your run-in with Stitch wasn't pleasant, but you have to remember, you were a threat to the club. It's his job to eliminate threats. Simple as that."

"Was Tristen a threat? Would he have eliminated her?"

"Tristen could never be considered a threat, child. She's a good kid with a lot of heart. We all think a lot of her."

"I hope you're right." My mind was filled with doubts. The not knowing was killing me.

"Big will find her. We'll know something by morning," he tried to assure me.

"By morning?"

"Take the pain medicine and get some sleep." He turned and walked out of the door. The room suddenly grew empty and cold, making me feel lost and alone. After taking one of the pills he'd given me, I pulled back the covers and crawled into bed. I closed my eyes. I wanted to forget what had happened, but my mind wouldn't let me. Every time I got close to falling asleep, a terrifying image would crash through my thoughts— the determined look in Stitch's eyes, the pain, the fear, and the panic. I tossed and turned for almost an hour, and then I remembered the last thing Doc told me: *by morning*. I couldn't help but wonder if Big had managed to dismantle the virus I'd used and was working on finding Tristen. Curiosity got the best of me, and I eased myself out of the bed. When I stepped out of the room, I had no idea where I was going. I had no idea which room was his, and the dark hallway was creeping me out. Ignoring that warning voice that was screaming in the back of my mind, I started walking quietly towards the end of the hall. I hadn't gotten very far when I noticed a hint of light shining from beneath one of the doors. Hoping that it might be his, I tapped on the door and waited.

"It's open."

The voice sounded familiar, deep and inviting, so I slowly cracked the door open. Relief washed over me when I found Big sitting at his computer, but when he turned to look at me with those beautiful gray eyes and body that most girls dream of, that feeling of relief was quickly replaced with a different feeling—a feeling I had no business feeling. He was sitting there with no shirt on – just a pair of loose fitting, low-rise shorts – and my mind went into sensory overload. So many muscles. And tattoos. And piercings. *Damn*. He was too hot for words. No man should look like that. It was so unfair, especially when I looked like a hot mess. And on top of that, there was the whole thing of him being a bad guy, a guy who might have hurt my sister—a guy I couldn't trust and certainly shouldn't lust after. Thankfully, those unwanted feelings quickly disappeared when I pulled my eyes away from his rock-hard abs over to his computer. When I caught a glimpse of my face on the screen, I felt like another bucket of cold water had been dumped over my head. "I see you got the server back up."

"I did."

"What are you doing?"

"I could ask you the same question. You should be in bed, or have you come to do some more voodoo shit to our server?"

"I couldn't sleep, and from what I can tell, it looks like you've taken care of all the voodoo."

"It wasn't easy, but I managed. How did you slip it in without me knowing it?"

"I slipped a worm into one of the emails I'd sent to Tristen."

"Smart. I'll give you that."

I walked over to him and saw that he'd found a picture of my father and me standing outside of MIT. I hadn't seen that picture in years and had no idea how he'd managed to find it. "So, now do you believe that I'm really Tristen's sister?"

"Never said I didn't, but proof never hurt."

"You should be trying to find Tristen. Not wasting time with this."

He crossed his arms as he turned his chair to face me. "Never been one to waste time, Josie. I've already checked into Tristen's flight. I know she never got on that second plane. I also know that neither she nor her friend Amanda checked into the hotel. I've got a contact looking into the security feed at the airport. If he finds anything, he'll let me know."

"Is he any good?"

"He's the best. I wouldn't have asked him otherwise."

His words hit me like a Mack truck. He believed me, and even after all I'd done, he was going to help me find my sister. He wasn't a bad guy after all, and for the first time since she'd gone missing, I had someone on my side willing to help find her. I'd wasted so much time thinking these men were the ones that had hurt Tristen. If I'd just trusted her, believed what she'd told me, then we would be closer to finding her. Thankfully, Big hadn't decided to hold my stunt against me and was still willing to help. I was surprised how much it meant to me. I could feel the emotions stirring inside of me as my eyes dropped to the floor. "Thank you."

"Come here." The sound of his voice was like a magnet pulling me towards him. Without thinking, I took that first step, only stopping when I was standing right in front of him. He placed his broad hands on my hips, easing me closer to him as he said, "I'm going to do whatever it takes to find your sister. You have my word on that."

"Okay."

"Now, go back to bed. You need to sleep."

I couldn't stomach the thought of going back to that room alone, so I asked, "Can I just stay in here?"

His hands fell from my hips as he considered my question. "Not sure that's a good idea."

"I won't bother you. I'll be quiet."

He sighed. "Just until I finish working on this. You can use the recliner. I sleep in it from time to time. It's not all that bad."

Relieved, I quickly walked over to the other side of the room and curled into his large, leather recliner. The intoxicating scent of his cologne surrounded me as I took the fleece blanket from the back of the chair and pulled it over me. I'd barely gotten settled when I heard him tapping away at his keyboard. I looked around the room, noting how different it was from Tristen's. Where her room was a bit girly, his was all man – gray walls, dark furniture, and a huge desk filled with every piece of technology you could imagine. From the looks of it, he spent most of his time sitting in front of his computer, just as he was now. I had no idea what time it was, but I knew it was late. He had to be tired, so I said, "You know it'd go a lot faster if you just told me what you were looking for."

"I thought you were going to be quiet."

"I'm just saying I could help." I rolled to my side and faced him. "Just tell me what you are trying to find."

"I need to fill in some of the blanks where Tristen is concerned. It could help us figure out where she might've gone."

"I can do that."

"After the car accident, she moved in with your Aunt Natalie?"

"Yes, but not at first. She started off with my grandmother, but it didn't work out. Tristen went through a bit of a wild streak. Skipped school. Stayed out late. Messed around with the wrong kids." It was hard knowing that my sister was spiraling out of control and there was nothing I could do about it. I remember trying to talk to her, but she just wouldn't listen. She was too angry and full of resentment, and I was the last person she wanted telling her what to do. My grandmother didn't know how to handle her, so she sent her to live with my aunt and uncle."

"And they lived in Seattle?"

"Yes. For as long as I can remember."

He turned back to face his computer. After typing for a few seconds, he asked, "How long did she stay with them?"

"Maybe six months. If that long. My uncle's always been a bit of a hard ass. He wouldn't take her crap, so she left. Ended up moving in with one of her friends. I never thought it was a good idea."

"What makes you say that?"

I yawned. As much as I hated it, the pills were starting to kick in. I closed my eyes as I answered, "She was too young to be out on her own."

"What do you know about Amanda?"

"Who?" I yawned again.

"The girl she went to Mexico with."

"She and Tristen worked at some diner. They lived together for a little while. She was a good kid…" I started. I was warm, I was beyond exhausted, and every word seemed hard to force out of my mouth. "She moved to LA about a year ago with her little sister," I yawned again, "Was surprised when Tristen… said… she was… going to Mexico with her." I heard him talking and even though I desperately wanted to hear what he was saying, it just sounded like a muddled mess of words. I could feel myself falling, and there was nothing I could do to stop it. My exhaustion finally won the battle, and I crashed.

Chapter 5

I've been dealt some shitty hands in the past, but this had to be one of the worst. She was lying there, looking so beautiful, so fucking tempting, and I couldn't do a damn thing about it. There was a time when things could've been different. I could've followed a different path, one more like hers – reputable and upstanding – but that wasn't the life I'd chosen. I liked things the way they were, but it didn't stop me from imagining what it would be like to have her wrapped in my arms. I knew I had a job to do, but every time I tried to focus on the computer screen, I found myself looking over at her. I couldn't help myself. I'd never known anyone like her. Sure, she was beautiful, but she was so much more than that. She was smart. She knew things and could do things that would make most people shake in their fucking boots. Her drive was a force to be reckoned with. Failure wasn't an option; either she would find a way or make one. I could see it in her eyes. There was a fire inside of her, not the kind that simmered deep inside, but the kind that flared and crackled for everyone to see, and I was drawn to it like a moth to a flame. I had to keep my distance or I was bound to get burned.

I had no idea what time it was until Cass knocked on my door. "Breakfast is almost ready."

Big

"Be there in a minute."

I got up and walked over to Josie. She looked so peaceful curled up in my recliner, and I hated to wake her. Reluctantly, I gave her a light nudge on the shoulder. "Josie?"

Her eyes fluttered open. "I must've dozed off." She stretched her arms above her head as she yawned. "I guess those pills were stronger than I thought."

"How ya feeling?"

"I'm okay." She stretched again, but this time her face twisted in pain.

"Doesn't look that way."

She winced once more as she tried to sit up in the chair. "I'm good. Just need a minute to get the kinks out."

She was trying to play it off, but I wasn't buying it. I knew she'd been through hell last night, and it was going to take her some time to get over it. "I'll get Doc to come check you out again."

"No need for that. I'm fine. Really." She feigned a smile as she brushed her hair out of her face. "Did you find out anything about Tristen?"

"Not yet."

"Any idea how long it will take to hear back from your guy?"

"Shouldn't be much longer. Thought we'd grab some breakfast while we wait. You hungry?"

After tossing the blanket to the side, she stood up and replied, "Yeah, I could go for something to eat."

"Then, we'll head down to the kitchen."

She looked down at her clothes and asked, "Wait… Shouldn't I change?"

"Up to you."

"You going to wait for me?"

"I can."

"Okay. Give me five minutes."

"Take your meds while you're down there."

She nodded, then rushed out the door. I'd barely had time to put on a t-shirt and jeans when she returned fully dressed and her hair pulled up in a messy bun. Simple, yet absolutely stunning. Damn. She was killing me.

"You ready?" she asked as she watched me put on my boots.

"I am now."

With her following close behind, I headed straight for the kitchen. When the loud rumble of laughter and talking came pouring out into the hall, Josie looked over at me with apprehension. "Sounds like a full house."

"Maybe, but it's nothing for you to worry about."

"That's easy for you to say. You do remember what happened last night. You know I haven't exactly had the warmest of welcomes so far."

I stopped and turned to face her. "We're all family here, Josie. We look out for each other. People say you can't choose your family, but they're wrong. We're brothers by choice. We've sworn a bond of brotherhood to each other, a bond stronger than blood, and there's nothing we won't do to keep our family safe. You came to us as a threat and never told us otherwise. We had to eliminate any chance of danger. You left us with no alternative."

"There's always another path."

"We will do whatever it takes to ensure the safety of our family, yesterday, tomorrow, and forever. Remember that. That should mean something to you when you think about your sister."

"That doesn't exactly make you any less scary," she mocked. "You're pretty intimidating with your tattoos, leather, and motorcycles. You're either right out of a horror flick or some girl's wet dream."

I couldn't help but laugh. "Wet dream, huh?"

She rolled her eyes. "I didn't say it was *my* wet dream."

"Mmm-hmm." I turned and started walking towards the kitchen. "They're good guys. You'll see."

When we walked in, everyone was already sitting down eating and talking. Josie was a bundle of nerves as she followed me over to the empty chairs and sat down. I'd tried to ease her worry, but it was obvious from the grim look on her face that my words hadn't made much of an impression. Her eyes skirted around the room as she checked out my brothers. Her eyes stopped on Cass. As always, she was buzzing around, making sure that everyone had what they needed. Her smile was contagious as she walked over to us.

"Help yourself, Hun." Cass smiled as she offered

Josie a plate. "Sorry, but the eggs are a little overdone."

I grabbed a plate and starting piling on the eggs, bacon, hash browns, and hot biscuits. "They'll be great. They always are."

Josie watched with curiosity as Cass poured me a fresh cup of coffee and placed it in front of me. "Have you been up all night?"

"No rest for the wicked."

"Any luck finding Tristen?"

"Not yet, but we're working on it." I loaded my fork with eggs and bacon before shoveling it into my mouth. I glanced over at Josie and was pleased to see she was doing the same.

Two Bit nudged me with his elbow as he motioned his head towards Josie. "That's Tristen's sister?"

"Yeah, that'd be her."

He leaned towards me, almost frothing at the mouth as he mumbled, "Damn. Good genes in that family. She's even hotter than Tristen."

An unexpected jolt of jealousy shot through me when I saw the way he was gawking at her. I didn't like the feeling—not one fucking bit. She was everything I'd ever wanted and knew I could never have. It was the story of my life, one that I'd grown accustomed to and wasn't about to start changing now – not even if it meant losing my one chance at something good. Choosing to ignore my spark of possessiveness, I looked over at Josie and said, "This big lug is Two Bit. Next to him is Q'. They're two of our newest members.

Big

Cass runs the bar and makes one hell of a breakfast. She's also Cotton's ol' lady." Josie's eyebrows furrowed with surprise. I can't say I blame her. Cass was much younger than Cotton and her bubbly personality was the polar opposite of Cotton's, but they worked. There was a real love between them, and together they kept us all on track. I motioned my head towards the end of the table. "And I'm sure you remember Maverick from last night, and that's Clutch beside him."

She lifted her hand to her head and gave them a quick salute. "Nice to meet you all."

They ignored the hint of sarcasm in her voice, and each took their turn greeting her. Once they'd all settled back down and started eating again, Clutch looked over to Josie with a smirk on his face. "So, the word is… you did a real number on Big yesterday. Pretty sure it's the first time anyone's ever gotten the upper hand on him."

She looked at me with a raised eyebrow. "I wouldn't say that. I am sitting here instead of being back at my apartment."

"Yeah, but you got a good jab in before he caught you. I mean, *damn*. No one does that shit to Big, and then you cut the power on top of that. I gotta say, I'm impressed."

"Umm… thank you?"

Before I could change the subject, Maverick asked, "How'd you do it?"

Her voice was low and flat, reminding me of

Charlie Brown's teacher as she replied, "I embedded a virus in one of Tristen's emails. Once he opened it, the security settings on his computer were lowered, and then the virus spread itself through your hard drive and server. From there, all your computers were sent a buffer filled with …"

"Damn." Maverick raised his hand, waving her off. "Forget I asked."

Clutch chuckled. "You didn't understand a damn thing she just said, did you?"

"Nope. Not a damn word, but I'm sure Big did. Bet that shit won't happen again."

"I used the fact that he was distracted against him. He was focused on trying to find out who I was, otherwise none of it would've worked."

I shook my head. "Maybe so, but you got me."

"But…"

I gave her a warning look, letting her know to drop it. The last thing I needed was her making fucking excuses for me. She'd gotten the better of me, and even though it irritated the hell out of me, I had to respect the fact that she was smart enough to pull that shit off. Thankfully, she picked up on the cue and let it go. She turned her attention back to her breakfast along with the rest of the guys. Just as we were finishing up, Wren walked into the kitchen. She tossed her purse on the counter with a loud, frustrated huff, then cursed under her breath as she stormed over to the sink to fill herself a glass of water. She didn't look like her typical self.

Big

Instead of the calm, laidback Wren we'd all grown accustomed to, we were faced with an irritated Wren who looked like she'd had one hell of a morning. Her eyes were red and teary, her cheeks were puffy, and her hair was a bit disheveled. I couldn't remember a time when I'd seen her so flustered. "You okay, Wren?"

She twirled around to face me with her eyebrow arched high. "No, I'm not. I'm pretty terrible in fact."

Cass got up out of her seat and rushed over to Wren. "What's going on? Is the baby okay?"

"She's fine. Still trying to get her to sleep through the night, but we're getting there. It's everything else that's driving me nuts…" Her voice trailed off.

"Like?" Cass pushed.

"Stitch, for one thing. His bad mood from last night spilled over into his morning, and his silence is about to drive me up the wall. I have no idea what went on here last night and I wouldn't dare ask, but let me tell you, my husband was not a happy camper when he got home." Wren leaned to the side and eyeballed me. "A little heads-up would've been nice."

"Got it. Heads-up next time."

"On top of that, there's this mess with Wyatt's teacher… I just don't know what else to do with her." Her voice quivered with worry as she leaned her back against the counter. "I know Wyatt is different, and I know that he's going to have his good days and his bad days, but this lady is making him absolutely miserable. He doesn't even want to go to school. It's like she's on him all the time. He is making wonderful grades, completes all his assignments, but she fusses at him for not paying attention. It's stuff like that all the time. It's wearing me out."

"Have you tried talking to her? Maybe if you explained…" Cass started.

"I have explained over and over again. I even explained it to the principal. I've never had issues like this. I hate the idea of moving him to another school, but I may not have any choice."

"Seems like she needs a little taste of her own medicine," Maverick growled. "Big, why don't you revoke her license?"

"Or foreclose on her house?" Two Bit suggested.

"Big, you should put her on a couple of those home delivery programs for some crazy shit like adult diapers and baby formula," Q' chuckled.

Maverick leaned back in his chair as he crossed his arms. "I was thinking he should donate her life's savings to one of the charities for Autism."

"No!" Wren scolded. "Big, leave her be. She's a new teacher and still has a lot to learn. One way or another, I'll figure it out."

"You sure?"

"Absolutely positive." She walked over to the table and took a seat next to Q'. "It's just hard when both of my guys are in a funk."

"Maybe it will be better today," Josie told her, sounding hopeful.

Big

Wren looked over at Josie with an apologetic look on her face. "I am so sorry. I didn't mean to carry on like that. Usually, I can keep it together a little better. I blame it on the lack of sleep." She extended her hand as she said, "You must be Josie."

"I am. It's nice to meet you, Wren."

"We're all worried about Tristen, but Big will find her. He's the best."

"Thanks, Wren. Hopefully, we'll get some news soon ..." Josie started, but stopped when she heard my phone ring with a text message.

I looked down at the screen and saw that Lenny, my contact, had finally gotten the video surveillance we were looking for. I looked over at Josie as I stood up. "He's got it."

"Has he sent it to you?"

"He is now."

She got up and started following me towards the door. Before we walked out, Maverick called, "Let us know what you find out."

Once we were in the hall, Josie asked, "Did he find anything?"

I could hear the desperation in her voice, and I wanted to give her good news. Unfortunately, I didn't have any to give. "He thinks he found her."

She followed me into my room and over to my computer. "Thank goodness."

I turned to face her, and seeing that hopeful look in her eye was like a punch to the gut. Lenny had already said it didn't look good, but he didn't give me any details. I had no idea what we were about to find on that video, and I needed her to be prepared for the worst. "Josie…"

"I know. You don't have to tell me."

"I just don't want you to get your hopes up. I have no idea what's on this file, but whatever it is, we'll get through it."

She looked up at me with determination in her eyes. "I'm going to hold you to that."

Chapter 6

Josie

I tried to think positively, tried not to imagine the worst, but as I watched Big open those files on his computer, all these horrific scenarios came crashing through my mind. It had already been six days. Anything could have happened to her, and I couldn't help but wonder if we were too late. I thought back to my parents' funeral, the pain I felt staring down at their graves, the emptiness I felt, and I couldn't imagine going through that again, not with my sister. I just couldn't do it. I was about to spiral into a pit of despair when my attention was drawn up to the three monitors mounted on Big's wall. Each screen showed a different angle of the surveillance video, allowing us to see everything that was happening in the airport. Eager to see if there was any sign of her, I leaned over Big's shoulder to get a better view. Hope washed over me when I spotted Tristen sitting at her gate. She was wearing her favorite hoodie with a pair of jeans, and there was a bright smile on her face. I could see the excitement in her eyes as she looked around at all the people passing by.

"There she is!"

"Mmm-hmm." Big reached for a chair and pulled it next to him. "Sit."

I was momentarily distracted by the authoritative tone in his voice. Surprisingly, I wasn't turned off by it, not even a little. In fact, a part of me actually liked it – along with the scent of his cologne and the way his bottom lip twitched when he tried to fight a smile. He was getting to me. My list of likes was slowly growing by the minute, but it didn't matter. As soon as I found my sister, I was getting the hell out of there.

When I realized I was still standing, I quickly sat down and looked back up at the screen. Lenny had gathered all the footage he could find of Tristen. There were twenty second lapses as the cameras scanned the other areas of the airport, but we still had a clear view of Tristen. We watched silently as she fiddled with her phone and played with her hair. Ten minutes had passed when a young blonde approached her. I assumed it was Amanda when Tristen jumped up and gave her a big hug. It wasn't until she turned around and sat down next to her that I realized it wasn't Amanda. At first I didn't recognize the woman, but there was something familiar about her. When I spotted the rose tattoo on her neck, it hit me. I knew exactly who she was. She'd changed a bit since I'd last seen her. Her brown hair was now platinum blonde with black tips and there were tattoos covering her left arm. She was much thinner than I remembered, and apparently she'd gotten herself a new set of boobs—big ones, but she still had that same shifty look about her. "That's not Amanda. It's her sister Lisa."

Big

When the footage skipped again, the time stamp at the bottom of the video showed that it was 7:45 pm. Tristen's flight was supposed to depart from Los Angeles at 8:30 pm. It was getting late, and there was no sign of Amanda. So many questions raced through my head, making me almost dizzy as I sat there hoping to find some answers. Neither Tristen nor Lisa seemed the least bit concerned about Amanda's absence as they got up and strolled over to one of the small coffee shops. The video blipped again, and Tristen was suddenly standing at the checkout line. Once they both placed their orders, they took their coffee and walked over to one of the tables. Tristen was just about to sit down, when she turned back towards the checkout counter.

Big nudged me softly with his elbow. "Did you catch that?"

"What?"

Big rewound the video several seconds and zoomed in on Lisa. "Keep your eyes on Lisa."

My focus had been totally on Tristen, so I missed it when Lisa slipped something out of her purse and dropped it into Tristen's coffee. "What was that?"

"Not sure. Looks like she might've drugged her. It would explain why Tristen was complaining about feeling dizzy."

"Drugged her? But why?" I took a deep breath. "Big, none of this is making any sense."

"I know, but we won't know anything until we see

how this plays out."

I couldn't take my eyes off the screen. It was like watching some horror flick as I watched my sister come back to the table with her dinner. She seemed so happy sitting there eating and talking, totally unaware that her life was in danger. It wasn't like Lisa had given her any signs that something was up. Instead, she acted all innocent and sweet, like they were the best of friends, and I hated her for it. I'd never felt such rage as I watched Tristen lift the cup up to her mouth and take another sip of coffee. I wanted to shout at her, warn her about Lisa, but it was too late. There was nothing I could do except sit there and watch.

"What else can you tell me about Amanda and Tristen? How long were they friends?"

"A couple of years I guess. They'd gotten close over the years. They looked out for one another. I always thought a lot of Amanda. She was there for Tristen when she really needed someone." My heart ached at the thought. When Tristen shut me out, I felt so lost. She was blinded by her resentment and never realized that I needed her just as much as she needed me. While I was glad that she had Amanda, it still hurt that she turned to her friends instead of me.

"Gotta wonder why she didn't show."

"It's not like her. Something must be wrong."

"What about Lisa? Any reason why she might wanna hurt Tristen? Some kind of grudge or something?"

Big

"Not that I know of… Honestly, none of this makes any sense. Lisa was a little rough around the edges, messed with the wrong crowd and ran into trouble from time to time, but I never dreamed she'd ever do something like this."

I looked up at the screen and watched as Tristen got up and emptied her tray into the garbage. Lisa followed her back to the waiting area and sat down. Tristen's smile quickly started to fade and a concerned look crossed her face. When she leaned back in her chair, I knew the drugs were starting to take their effect. She looked panicked as she reached into her purse and took out her phone.

Big looked over at me and said, "This must be when she called you."

I checked the time at the bottom of the screen and saw that it read 8:25. "I think so, but we can check my phone records to be sure."

While she was still talking on the phone, she stood up and started walking towards the bathroom. As soon as she was gone, Lisa took out her phone and sent a text message to someone. My eyes widened as I watched her grab Tristen's bags and head towards the bathroom. Moments later, she came out of the bathroom with Tristen leaning against her. Tristen's arm was wrapped around her shoulder, and her eyes were barely open. She could hardly walk as Lisa led her out of their terminal and towards the front of the airport.

"What is she doing?" I whispered to myself. I

couldn't believe what I was seeing. Tristen stumbled several times, almost falling flat on her face, and not one person asked if they needed any help. No one even attempted to stop them. They just sat there silently as Lisa tugged my helpless sister out of the airport and to the pick-up lane. Lisa stopped at the curb and waited as a black SUV pulled up. A tall, muscular Hispanic man got out of the passenger side of the truck and walked to the rear of the vehicle. After he opened the back door, Lisa shoved Tristen inside. I felt the air rush out of my lungs when she slammed the door shut, trapping my sister inside. I brought my hands to my face, covering my mouth as I muttered, "Oh, God. Where are they taking her?"

Knowing I was about to lose it, Big placed his hand on my thigh and gave me a gentle squeeze. I looked down at my leg, surprised how comforting a simple touch could be, especially from a man like him. He seemed so strong, so self-assured, and yet there was a gentle side to him, a side I couldn't help but find appealing. "I can't make you any promises, Josie... but I give you my word, I'll do everything I can to bring her back home."

I placed my hand on his as I said, "I know you will."

After a quick nod, he turned his attention back to the man on the screen. "Have you seen him before?"

"No. Never." There was no way I could ever forget a man like that. His jet-black hair was combed back away from his face, revealing his cold, black eyes. Tattoos covered his arms, hands, and neck, but these were nothing like Big's tattoos. His were ominous and threatening, just like the rest of him. And there was something about the number tattooed on his neck that caught my attention. I knew very little about gangs, but I figured their ink held some kind of importance. Something told me we weren't dealing with just some thug off the street.

"Let's see if our facial recognition software will bring anything up on him." Big took a screenshot of the man's face and plugged it into the program. We both waited silently to see if we could get a hit on the photo. After forty-five minutes of searching, Big stopped the program. "Let's try a different angle."

He took a new, clearer picture and uploaded it onto his computer. Once he had it up and running, he leaned back in his chair and stared up at the screen. When several pictures popped up on the screen, I leaned forward to get a better look. "It's him!"

"Victor Aguilera, aka El Toro."

"It says he's a member of Calaveras de la Muerte."

"He is."

"That's the Mexican cartel." Panic surged through me. "That's bad, right?"

With little expression on his face, Big stood up and started for the door. "Need a word with Cotton. Go through the video again. See if you pick up anything we might've missed. When I get back, we'll see what we can find out about Amanda."

"But, what about Victor?"

"Check the video, Josie." His voice was hard and cold, and I could see from the tense look on his face that he was concerned. I wanted him to talk to me, to tell me what was running through his head, but he cut me off and left me to worry alone, making me freak out even more.

I tried to push back all the emotions swirling inside me as I scooted over into his chair. I had to focus and couldn't let my doubts stand in the way of finding my sister. I went through the film for a second time, making sure I didn't miss a single detail, but ended up with more questions than answers. I couldn't help but wonder if Amanda had some part to play in Tristen's kidnapping. I tried calling her more times than I could count, but she never answered. Maybe they'd gotten her too, but it seemed unlikely. I couldn't imagine why Lisa would put her sister in danger like she had mine. My frustration level was reaching an all-time high, so I turned my focus back to the video. I scanned back to the SUV.

No matter how much I zoomed in, I couldn't make out who was behind the wheel, but I was able to get the license plate number. Just as I was about to start searching for the owner of the vehicle, Big returned. The expression on his face was a tad intimidating as he walked over to me. "Is everything okay?"

"As well as it can be. You find something?"

Big

"I got the license plate off the SUV."

"That's good." He sat down beside me and leaned back in his chair. "Let's see what we can find out."

He waited patiently as I started my search. When the results came up, I knew we'd reached a dead end. "It's registered to a Louise Carlton. An eighty-year-old woman from Nebraska."

"Stolen plate."

"Now what?"

"Let's see what we can find on Lisa."

After forty-five minutes of searching, I came up empty handed. "I can't find anything. No home address. No phone number. It's like she vanished after she left Washington."

"You said she moved to LA with her sister, right?"

"As far as I know, she did. Maybe everything is under Amanda's name."

"You got an address for her?"

I couldn't think. It was too much. All of it. The video. Lisa. Victor. The Mexican cartel. How in the world would we ever get my sister back? The worry I felt was all-consuming, making it impossible for me to get a hold of my fear, and I could only imagine what my sister must have been feeling.

Chapter 7

"Shit." There was no mistaking the panic in her voice. We'd all heard the horror stories about the cartel, the brutality, the heartless murders over drugs and family wars, and we knew there was no way our club had the power to go up against them. "We have to go to the police."

"The police?" I laughed. "What the hell are they going to do about it?"

"They can go in there and arrest them. They'll get my sister back!"

She'd lost her damn mind. There was no way in hell we could go to the police with this. They were the last people I'd trust to get Tristen out of there. "It's a gang, Josie. The cops can't do shit. You gotta know that."

"Why? It's their job! That's what they are there for!"

"No."

"They've got to do something. We'll show them the video. That's all the proof they need."

"You got two girls sitting in an airport. They hug. They talk. They spend over an hour together with no sign that anything is wrong. Then, one of them gets a little sick, and they decide to leave. End of story.

Big

You've got no proof that anyone did anything wrong."

"*Are you kidding me*? She put something in her drink!"

"Could have been anything. Sugar even."

"Big! You know that's not what happened!" she shouted. She was getting pissed, but I needed her to see why we couldn't go to them.

"You're not hearing me, Josie. We can't trust the cops with this. For every good cop, there are two bad." She turned to face me with her eyes full of intensity. "These people even hear we're asking about Tristen, and they *will kill her*."

Having her so close was screwing with my head. Everything about her, from the scent of her hair to the tiny freckles on the bridge of her nose, was driving me to the edge. I needed to stay focused, but the undeniable pull I felt towards her was making it impossible for me to concentrate. I couldn't take the way she looked at me, like I had all the answers, like I was some kind of fucking hero who was going to save the day. I wanted to be that hero for her, to give her whatever she needed, but in the end, I'd only let her down. Even if I managed to bring her sister home, I'd never be a fucking hero. I'd never be the kind of man a girl like Josie deserved, so I had to forget about making her mine and find Tristen. Finding her was the only thing that mattered.

Tears streamed down her face. "What are we going to do?"

I placed my hand on hers. "I know it's hard, but

you've gotta trust me on this, Josie. We'll figure something out."

I couldn't tell her, but I knew it in my gut that we were fucked. That's all there was to it. We were royally, unbelievably *fucked*. The minute I saw the ink on that guy's neck, I knew we were in trouble. Everyone knew the Mexican cartel was growing rampant in southern California, and while I'd never dealt with them directly, I knew the men who belonged to these organizations were ruthless. There was nothing they wouldn't do to protect their livelihood. The narcotics they distributed were some of the purest around and went for higher prices. They played it smart. By laying low and staying in rural areas, they were able to divide out the drugs and distribute them without getting caught. Unfortunately for us, they didn't just deal with drug distribution. Sex trafficking was also a huge money maker for them. From everyday prostitution to high-end slavery, there was always a market for sex. Once they had a guy willing to pay the right price, they'd find a way to make it happen, even if that meant kidnapping a girl in an airport.

There was only one person I knew who could help us. He'd spent his life developing contacts, making connections with the shadiest to the savviest, and lucky for us, he owed me a favor. I took my phone from my back pocket and sent him a message. After he responded, I forwarded the video footage to my email and reached for my cut. "I'll be back in a couple of hours."

"Wait! Where are you going?" She hopped up from her seat and took a step towards me.

"Got someone I need to see. Think he might be able to help us." I grabbed my keys, then started for the door.

"Are you leaving me here?"

"Yeah. I'll be back as soon as I can. You can wait for me in Tristen's room or go meet up with the girls at the bar or something."

With a determined look on her face, she took another step towards me. "No."

"No?"

"*No*. I'm going with you." She took one of my hoodies off the coatrack and slipped it over her head. The hem of the sweatshirt fell at her knees, making her look even smaller. "All set."

"*Josie…*"

"I'm just going along for the ride. I'll keep my mouth shut."

"I've heard that before."

"Seriously. I won't say a word. I just need to get out of here for a little bit and get some fresh air… Let me tag along. *Please*."

"You're gonna need a coat and gloves. Go grab some out of Tristen's closet and meet me out front."

Without another word, she headed out the door and down the hall. On my way out, I stopped by Cotton's office. Early on, we'd both agreed that going to war with the Calaveras wasn't an option, so we'd have to come up with another way to get Tristen back. When I told him my plans to go see Nitro, he had his doubts, but ultimately gave me the okay. When I finally made it outside, the lot was basically empty. Most of the guys were either out on this month's run, or they were working in the garage. I started towards my bike and found Josie already standing there waiting for me. She was all bundled up like a damned Eskimo with Tristen's helmet in her hand. Most women would've kept a man waiting, fixing their hair or making sure their makeup was on just right, but Josie wasn't like most women. She had her mind set, determined and undistracted, and nothing was going to slow her down, especially not her damned hair. I liked that about her.

"Clutch told me this was your bike."

"It is."

Her nose crinkled as she smiled. "He said that I was gonna freeze my ass off."

"You might." I put on my helmet and threw my leg over the seat. "You can always stay here."

"I'll be fine." It took her a minute to get her helmet on, but once it was on, she eased her leg over the seat. She grimaced slightly from the pull on her sore muscles, but she shook it off and settled in behind me. After she put her feet up on the foot pegs, she patted me on my lower thigh. "All set."

I felt like a damn horse being told to giddy-up with that damn pat, but it worked. Without hesitation, I started the engine and headed out of the gate. Nitro was waiting for me at one of the old dive bars out by the dock, so it wasn't exactly a quick ride. At first, Josie kept her hands tightly clamped around my waist. She was rigid and tense, especially when we took a curve, but eventually she acclimated herself. Her hands slowly drifted to my hips, and she started to relax a little. When we got out onto the main road, the cold wind kicked up, making me think I should've taken a cage, but she didn't complain. Instead, she pressed her chest against my back, tucking her head against my shoulder. Fuck. She was so close. Why did she have to feel so damn good wrapped around me? It was like her body was made for mine, and I liked it. I liked it too much, and under different circumstances, I would've taken the long way to Nitro's. Unfortunately, that wasn't an option. Nitro was expecting us, and he wasn't a man who liked to wait.

When I pulled up to the bar, I killed the engine and waited for Josie to get off the bike. She placed her hands on my shoulder and eased herself off. She took a step back and looked around with confusion. The parking lot was basically empty, and the dark windows made it look like no one was inside. "Is this place even open?"

Without responding, I took my helmet off and put it on the seat. After she'd done the same, I started walking towards the door. Before we stepped inside, I turned to her. "Mouth shut."

She sighed with acceptance and nodded as she followed me inside. Nitro was sitting at one of the tables in the back, and he gave me a curious look when he spotted Josie walking behind me. "You didn't tell me you were bringing a tag-along with you."

"This is Josie, Tristen's sister."

A mischievous grin crossed his face as he gave her the once-over. "Hey there, beautiful. Just seeing you has brightened my day."

Nitro was a cocky bastard, but his arrogance was expected. In his profession, you had to be a self-confident prick. The people he dealt with would consider any sign of weakness a death sentence, and Nitro knew it. He was one of the best. It'd taken him a long time and lots of hard hits, but he'd established himself in the gun trafficking world. Even though he was tough, deep down he was a good guy; I wouldn't have come to him if he wasn't.

She offered him her hand and said, "Wish I could say the same."

"Ahhh, got yourself a fiery one here, Big. I like her." He motioned us both to sit down. "I gotta say, I was surprised to hear that you needed my help. It's usually the other way around."

"Wouldn't have taken your time unless it was important." I waited for Josie to take a seat, and then I sat down in front of Nitro. "Tristen's missing."

"Got any idea where she might be?"

"I do. That's why we're here." I reached for my phone and pulled up the video. "Watch this."

He took the phone from my hand and started to

skim through footage from the airport. "Fuck, brother."

"Exactly."

He looked over at me, and it was clear he was rattled. "You know what you're dealing with here?"

"I do. That's why I came to you. I need your help with this, brother. The club can't go up against the fucking cartel. We need another way to get our girl back."

"Not sure what I can do here." He ran his fingers through his short, dark hair. "I can make some calls. See what I can find out."

"That's all I'm asking."

"I'll do what I can. It's gonna take some time. Until I get back to you, keep your mouth shut. Don't go asking around or digging into these guys. Don't do a fucking thing, Big. The last thing we want to do is tip them off. They'll kill us and her without blinking a fucking eye."

"Understood."

"Give me 'til morning."

"Until morning?" Josie complained. "But, we need to know something now."

I looked over at her with a warning look. *"Josie."*

As expected, she ignored me and continued her rant. "You obviously know your way around these kinds of people or Big wouldn't have brought us here. A few hours could make the difference between us getting her back or losing her forever."

"Beautiful and speaks her mind. I like it." He

chuckled. "I'll do what I can."

I stood up and motioned for Josie to do the same. "Time to go."

With a defeated look on her face, Josie got up and started walking away from the table. Before she stepped out the door, Nitro called out to her. "Josie."

She turned to face him. "Yes?"

"I'll do what I can. I give you my word."

The tension in her face diminished as she replied, "Thank you, Nitro."

Once we were back to the bike, I stood angrily as I watched Josie slip on her helmet. When she noticed my expression, her eyes dropped to the ground. "I'm sorry."

"You can't do that shit, Josie. When I say keep your mouth shut, that's exactly what I expect you to do. Period."

"But…"

"No fucking buts about it. This isn't some game. This is the real deal. Lives are at stake, including yours and mine. Nitro isn't a man that does fucking favors, Josie. This shit is gonna cost me. You don't have to understand it. You don't have to like it. But you do have to do what you're told. You got it?"

"What do you mean it's gonna cost you?"

"And you don't ask fucking questions!"

"Fine! But, you don't have to be a total asshole about it!"

"Apparently, I do, 'cause you don't listen for shit!" I grabbed my helmet and put it on. "Now, get your ass on the bike and zip it."

"You're a dick." She took off her helmet and tossed it on the ground as she started walking away from me.

She'd only taken a step when I reached for her and pulled her to me. Surprise filled her eyes as I took a step forward, pinning her to the back wall of the bar. I could feel the heat of her breath against my neck as I held her there. She looked up at me with a mix of determination and lust in her eyes. "You're right. I am a dick. I am an asshole, but I'm here. I'm doing what I can to save your sister and protect you in the process. It's not exactly easy when you don't do what I tell you to."

She slowly exhaled as she considered what I'd just said. "I'm sorry. You're right, and you're not an asshole."

"I am. I'm not one of the good guys, Josie."

"I kinda think you are."

"You're wrong. Dead wrong."

Having her so close to me was making my entire body ache with need. I wanted her. There was no denying that, and seeing that same craving reflected back at me made it impossible to resist her. Without thinking of the consequences, I leaned into her.

Just as I was about to press my mouth against her perfect full lips, the back door slung open and our attention was quickly drawn over to Nitro.

"I think I may have something." The moment was lost as we both took a step back and waited for him to continue. "I'm still working on it, but I know who has her. My contact thinks she's with a crew in southern California. He's going to do some checking and get back to me in a couple of hours."

"Any idea what these guys are planning to do with her?"

He paused for a moment, looking at Josie with concern before he answered, "I don't know yet, but I'm sure it isn't good."

"What does that mean?"

"It means we gotta play it smart. These guys don't fuck around, but then, neither do I."

Chapter 8
Josie

My mother once told me that falling for the wrong man was like jumping off a cliff. When you hit rock bottom, you'll end up broken with scars that last a lifetime. I knew Big was just the kind of man she was talking about. Everything about him screamed wrong—hacker, member of a motorcycle club, leather and tattoos, criminal—but something about him kept pulling at me. It had been over an hour since I left him, and I could still feel the warmth of his body pressed against mine, could still smell the scent of his cologne on my skin, and could still feel that rush I felt when he was about to kiss me. I was walking on the edge of that cliff, and I feared I might just take a running leap. As much as I wanted to know what it would be like to be loved by him, I knew it would be a mistake. I had no place in his world, nor he in mine. We were wrong for each other in every way. I had to keep my distance and stay focused on finding my sister. I needed to forget those gnawing feelings I had growing in the pit of my stomach. They would only cause me trouble, and more trouble was the last thing I needed.

I turned on my side and tried to find a comfortable position. Unfortunately, the throbbing in my muscles was becoming worse, making it harder to ignore. I looked over at the bottle of pills on the bedside table and decided to take one in hopes of easing some of the pain. After an hour, the aching finally subsided, but I still couldn't sleep. It was only eight o'clock, and where Big was exhausted from being up all night, I was wide awake. I turned on the TV and tried to find something to watch, but had no luck. The longer I lay there, the harder it was to ignore the voices in my head, especially Nitro's. When he talked about those men and their plans for my sister, my blood ran cold. Just thinking about the nonchalant way he spoke about the cartel made my skin crawl. I'd never met anyone like him. While he was attractive with his tousled brown hair and hazel eyes, a sense of power radiated off of him, making him seem more than a little threatening. But when he smiled and the light sparkled in his beautiful hazel eyes, I could see there was a different side to him, one that was kind and trustworthy, making me understand why Big would be friends with a man like him. I just hoped that together they'd be able to find a way out of this mess.

I couldn't think about it anymore. I felt like the walls were closing in on me, and I had to get out of there, even if it was just to get something to eat from the kitchen. I hoped the taste of something sweet would settle my nerves and help me get some much needed sleep. Just as I opened the door, I found Big standing there—with no shirt on *again*—looking hot as ever. Damn. The man was killing me. "Hey."

"You okay?" His voice sounded like he'd just

woken up, low and raspy and sexy as hell.

"Yeah, I'm fine. Why?"

He leaned against the door as he yawned. "Just checking."

"I thought you were going to get some sleep."

"I was. Got hungry." I sighed silently to myself as he smiled and ran a hand over his chiseled stomach. I didn't stand a chance.

"I was thinking the same thing."

"Wanna go to the kitchen and grab a bite?"

All those thoughts of keeping my focus shot out the window when I answered, "Sure. Sounds good."

When I stepped out into the hall, his lips curled into a smirk when he noticed what I was wearing. It was cold in Tristen's room, really cold. It's the only reason why I'd put back on his hoodie. Besides, it was comfortable with the leggings I'd borrowed from Tristen. It had absolutely nothing to do with the fact that it smelled like him or it gave me a sense of comfort to have close to my skin – absolutely nothing. Choosing to ignore the goofy look on his face, I stepped past him and headed down the hall. When we got into the kitchen, Big went straight for the fridge. "Whatcha in the mood for?"

"Depends on what you've got."

"There's leftover burgers from dinner... some sandwich stuff..." He paused as he walked over to the cabinets. "Cereal and Pop-Tarts."

I walked over to him, and when I noticed a box of

my favorite kid's cereal, I grabbed it. "This will do."

"Got enough in there for two bowls?"

I gave it a good shake and answered, "Yep. Plenty."

"Good."

He took the milk from the refrigerator and got us some bowls and spoons before heading over to the table. We both poured ourselves a giant helping and ate in silence. When his bowl was almost empty, he reached for the box and poured himself another large helping. The silence starting to get to me, I asked, "So... where'd ya learn so much about computers?"

"Taught myself."

"Seriously?" It wasn't a secret that lots of kids learned about the elements of hacking on their own, especially during the era when Big grew up. The World Wide Web was new and had limited security, opening them up to limitless opportunity. It was a kind of sport to them, pushing a boundary or learning cool new tricks to brag about. It wasn't like that for me. I'd spent hours upon hours watching my father, learning everything he knew about technology. His passion for the computer world was ingrained in me from an early age, and I was always eager to learn more. It was one of the reasons why I'd decided to study information systems in college. I loved it, and I was finally at the point where I could do just about anything with processors and coding. What had taken me years to accomplish with my father's help and tons of classes, Big had learned on his own, which was pretty freaking impressive.

Big

"Had some help along the way."

"From Nitro?"

He chuckled under his breath. "Nitro doesn't know shit about computers."

"Then, how did you two meet?"

He hesitated for a moment, studying me before he gave his answer. "Met him in prison."

"Oh." I could hear my mother's voice chanting "wrong, wrong, wrong" as I thought about all the things he could've done—maybe he killed someone or he was dealing drugs or he robbed a bank. The list was endless, and my mind was racing with curiosity as I took another spoonful of my cereal. I knew it was none of my business, but I couldn't stop myself from asking. "And... why exactly did you end up in prison?"

"Which time?"

I looked up at him, noting the playful look in his eyes, and it was clear he was mocking me. "Which time? Really?" He just shrugged his shoulders and smiled. "Ok, then. Let's go with the first time."

"Got sent to juvie for hacking into my dad's trucking service. At first, I just wanted to check his schedule so I'd know where he was going and when he'd be back. It wasn't a big deal until I started messing with his route."

"Why would you mess with his route?"

"Heard my folks talking about money troubles. My dad was gonna have to find a second job unless something changed. So, I swapped some stuff around.

Got him some longer routes with a higher pay grade. Things were going fine until one of the guys started bitching about his cut in pay. They looked into it, found out what I was doing, and off to juvie I went."

"And your dad?"

"He lost his job and pretty much blamed me for fucking everything up."

"But, you were only trying to help."

"He didn't see it that way." As soon as the words left his mouth, it was like someone jerked him a hundred miles away. He was completely lost in his own thoughts as he ate the rest of his cereal.

I should've just left it, but I didn't. "And the other time?"

He leaned back in his chair. "By the time I got out of juvie, things at home had changed, and not for the better. My folks were always at each other's throats, bitching about this or that, and I knew things were about to fall apart. When my dad would go out in the truck, my mom would all but disappear. For days, I wouldn't hear anything from her. Knew something was up, so I decided to check into it and see where she was going. I hacked into the phone company and searched her call history and tracked her phone. Found out she was cheating with some guy from her office. I threatened to tell Dad, and instead of ending things with the guy, she called the cops and told them what I'd done. I ended up spending a year and half in prison."

"You've got to be kidding me. Your own mother

turned you in? That's crazy."

"Yeah, well crazier shit has happened. When I got out of jail, I left my life as Michael Davis behind and started over."

The hurt in his eyes pulled at me, so I placed the palm of my hand on top of his. "I'm really sorry."

He pulled his hand from mine as he crossed his arms and said, "Nothing to be sorry about. In the end, everything turned out the way it was meant to. This is where I belong."

"I guess, but it seems like a hard way to get where you're going."

"Sometimes the hard way is the only way to go."

"What about Nitro? What did he go in for?"

He shrugged. "No idea."

"You were in jail together for a year and a half, and he never told you why he was there?"

"Nope. That's the thing about Nitro; he knows when to keep quiet. It's one of the reasons he's been able to do as well as he has. People trust him to keep his mouth shut." His lips curled into a mischievous grin. "It's a talent *some* people don't have."

He looked at me with a sexy little smirk. I shook my head and rolled my eyes. "The man has jokes."

"From time to time." He got up and took our empty bowls to the sink. "I figure Nitro wouldn't have gotten put away unless he wanted to."

"What do you mean?"

"He went in as a small fish in a big, fucking pond.

Came out with new connections, new clientele, and now he's one of the biggest damn fish out there."

"So, you think he went to jail on purpose?"

"I always thought so."

"That's pretty screwed up. You know that, right?"

"Maybe, but it worked." He stretched his arms above his head as he yawned.

Remembering that he still hadn't slept, I reached for the box of cereal and took it back over to the cabinet. Once I'd shut the door, I looked over at him and said, "I guess I should let you get some sleep."

He nodded and followed me down to Tristen's room. I opened the door, and just as I was about to step inside, Big said, "I've got something to tend to tomorrow."

"Okay." I wanted to ask him where he was going, but stopped myself when I remembered our argument from earlier. He'd made it clear that I wasn't supposed to ask questions, so I kept my mouth shut.

"I'll have Cass come by in the morning. Maybe she can run you over to your place to get some of your stuff."

A thrill shot through me when I thought about going back home, but it was short-lived. I quickly realized going home would mean leaving the clubhouse and my only real connection to my sister, so I decided I didn't want to leave. I told myself I wanted to stay because of Tristen, but in my heart, I knew she wasn't the only reason. "That would be great."

Big

"Good. I'll check in on you when I get back."

He paused for a moment, staring at me with a heated look, and then, without another word, he turned to leave. Disappointment washed over me as I watched him walk down the hall. As much as I hated myself for it, I wasn't ready for him to go and had to fight the urge to call him back. I knew I needed to guard my heart and keep my distance, but each time I was around him, I lost a little of my resolve. Before I did something I would regret, I quickly shut the door and crawled back into bed. I pulled the covers close around me, snuggling and trying to settle the storm of thoughts that kept spiraling in my head. Tristen. Big. The Calaveras. Nitro. The club. It was all too much. Thankfully, between my full stomach and the pain medication, I didn't have any trouble falling asleep.

Chapter 9
Big

I was beyond exhausted, but sleep just wouldn't come. I tossed and turned, but nothing could get her out of my head. Our conversation about my past kept playing in my mind. I meant it when I said there was nothing for her to feel sorry about. I'd made my own choices, and the consequences were mine to bear. Surviving the hard times let me know what I was made of and how much hell I could really take. Between jail, Baker and his thugs, and all the other shit in-between, I learned early on I could take a hell of a lot. Each time I was knocked down, I learned to build myself back up, make myself even stronger, smarter, and in the end, I survived and I'm living the life I wanted to live. That's all that matters. I'm not sure a girl like her could ever get that, especially when everything had been laid out on a red carpet. She'd had her hard times, but the real test – the one that would determine what she was really made of – was yet to come.

I had an early meet with Nitro to discuss what he'd uncovered, so I did my best to clear my head and get some sleep. I'd barely dozed off when my alarm went off. I jumped in the shower and headed out. The sun was just starting to rise when I pulled out of the gate and headed over to Nitro's place. There was no way of knowing what he'd found out, so I didn't bother telling Josie where I was headed. If he'd gotten bad news, he'd just blurt it out. It wasn't his style to sugarcoat anything, so I figured it would be best for me to come alone. When I walked into his office, he was leaned back in his chair sipping on a cup of coffee.

His feet were propped up on the desk and his ball cap was pulled down low, covering his tired eyes. He looked down at his watch and shook his head. "It's too damn early for this shit."

I took the seat in front of him. "Figured you'd been up for hours."

"I have been." He took a long drink of his coffee. "Still too damn early."

"Quit whining and let me know what you found out."

He dropped his feet to the floor and sat up in his chair. "My guy said they've got some big buyers coming into LA in a couple of weeks."

"What kind of buyers?"

"The kind looking to buy themselves a pretty, blue-eyed blonde. These guys come from all over the world and are willing to pay a pretty hefty price for the right girl."

"You think that's what they're planning to do with Tristen?"

"She has the look they want."

"But how can we be sure that's what they're planning?"

"There's no way to be one hundred percent without seeing her for ourselves, but my guy had connections to Victor Aguilera, and he has a girlfriend named Lisa."

"Damn."

"They've got her. I feel it in my gut."

"Any idea where they're keeping her?"

"Nikko thinks they've got her holed up in Santa Fe Springs, a town close to LA. They'll have her hidden away in some warehouse or a member's home. Figure they've got her pretty heavily drugged and guarded around the clock."

"This is crazy, brother."

"Yeah, but there's money in this shit, Big. Lots of it. Some of these girls go for up to three hundred grand." He finished off his cup of coffee and reached in his pocket for his pack of cigarettes. After lighting one up, he continued, "The buyers will expect their girls to be unmarked, so I figure they'll treat them differently than the girls they use for their prostitution ring. That's a good thing for Tristen."

I didn't see anything good about it. The thought of Tristen chained to a bed and drugged out of her mind made me sick to my stomach. She was a good kid and deserved better than that shit. Hell, a damn dog deserved better than that shit. "How do we get her out?"

"We don't. Not without a war."

"War isn't an option, Nitro. We don't have the kind of manpower we'd need to go up against them, not for something like this."

Big

"There is one thing we could try," he started as he took another puff from his cigarette. "I've got some connections. I could use them to get in on the auction. I'll do whatever it takes to get the highest bid and ..."

I leaned forward in my chair as I finished his sentence. "Buy her?"

"Yep. That's what I was thinking. We could just pay them outright. It's the only chance we have to bring her home without causing some rift."

"I don't know, Nitro. That shit sounds pretty fucking risky, and that's a lot of money."

"Maybe so." He placed his elbows on his desk and smoke billowed around him as he leaned towards me. "But have you got any better ideas?" When I didn't answer, he snickered. "Me either. They'll bring the girls into LA for the auction in four days. That gives us a little time to get things prepared. Until then, we lay low. If they have any idea what we are up to, we're all dead."

"I gotta run this thing by Cotton." I stood up and started towards the door.

"Knew you would. Tell him I've got it covered."

"Will do." I remembered I hadn't gotten back to him about the new contacts, so before I walked out, I said, "Forgot to get back to you about your boys. Tate is legit, but Ballard doesn't feel right. Give me a little more time with him."

"I'll touch base with Tate. Thanks, brother."

"Anytime." I headed out to the parking lot and got on my bike. We'd had another shipment going out, so I knew Cotton would be working in the office for most of the day. Since he was expecting to hear from me, I headed straight there to fill him in on what Nitro had uncovered. As expected, when I walked into the office, he was sorting through a stack of files. I walked over to him and asked, "Got a minute?"

"Got a few." He placed a file down on his desk as he leaned back in his chair. "What did you find out from Nitro?"

I could see the disgust creep across Cotton's face as I repeated everything Nitro had told me about Tristen and the Calaveras. Once I was done, he leaned against the counter and growled, "Fuck."

"It's not perfect, but it could work. It's a lot of money."

Cotton didn't even bat an eye when I brought up how much it could cost to get Tristen back. The club has always done well, money was always there if we needed it, and if spending a shit ton now meant keeping us out of war, Cotton wouldn't think twice about it. "You're right. The plan isn't perfect, but it's the only chance we've got of getting our girl back. Do what needs to be done. Money isn't an object. Tell Nitro we've got it covered."

"The auction is a few days away. We'll head out tomorrow night to make sure we've got everything covered."

"Good. Get with Stitch. Fill him in on all the details and let him know when you plan to leave. Get Maverick too, if you think you'll need him."

"We'll be good with just Stitch. Nitro is bringing a couple of his guys along, too. We don't want to draw any unnecessary attention."

"Let me know if you change your mind." He ran his hand along the base of his neck. "You got plans for Josie while you're in LA?"

The thought of leaving her behind hadn't even crossed my mind, so I replied, "She's going."

He looked surprised by my response. "Not sure that's a good idea, brother."

"I do. We're gonna need someone like her. Someone who has the skill set to monitor camera feeds and radio frequencies while we're on the inside."

"You think she can handle it?"

"I do."

"Then she'll be your responsibility. Make sure she has whatever she needs. And so we are clear, I don't want any of this to come back and bite us in the ass."

"Understood."

I was about to turn to leave when he said, "If you've got a minute, see if you can help Two Bit out in the garage. His little project has been giving him some trouble."

I nodded and headed out to the garage. When I walked in, I found Two Bit with his head still crammed under the hood of the cream colored 1947 Buick Super. It was hard to believe it was the same car he and Q' had brought in a few months back. Back then, it was a rusted, ragged-out piece of shit, but they did a complete overhaul on it. Now, it was a real beauty. "You need a hand?"

He growled, "I'm about to lose it on this damn thing."

Two Bit had his talents, like breakdowns, sanding, and anything that dealt with hard, physical labor, but engine work was not one of his strong suits. "Let me take a look."

We spent the next three hours working on her, and once we were done, she purred like a kitten. Two Bit smiled like a kid on Christmas morning as he sat behind the wheel and revved the engine. "Sounds good, don't ya think?"

"Perfect."

He was still smiling when he killed the engine and got out of the car. "Thanks for the help, brother. I owe you one."

"Anytime."

I was just about to leave when he waltzed over to me with a cheesy grin. "So, what's the deal with Tristen's sister?"

He was interested in her. There was no mistaking it. I couldn't blame him. She was beautiful without letting it get to her head, classy but not too classy, and smart without needing to prove it. And that sexy little lopsided grin of hers didn't hurt things either. I understood his interest, but that didn't mean I liked it. "Leave it, brother."

"Whoa, man. I didn't know." He took a step back and raised his hands in surrender. "If you had a thing for her, all you had to do was say the word."

I had no claim to her. Hell, I hadn't even kissed her. I knew I had no right to tell him to fuck off, but the words just rolled off my lips. "Consider it said."

"Well, I'll be damned." He slapped me on the back and smiled. "Big Mike's done gone and got himself a girlfriend."

"Shut it, Two Bit," I told him as I turned and headed for the door. "Not in the mood for your bullshit. Besides, it's time for you to get started on the Ford."

He chuckled under his breath. "On it."

I was still cursing myself when I got back to my room. The last thing I needed was my brothers thinking I had a thing for Josie. She wasn't mine, and it was a waste of time thinking she ever would be. The thought tore at me, making me wish things could be different. I had to pull my head out of my ass and remember that I was there to help get her sister home. Nothing more. Nothing less. Too bad that was easier said than done.

Chapter 10
Josie

When Big told me that Cassidy was going to run me by my apartment, he didn't mention that her sister Henley and her nephew Thomas would be tagging along. I was a little nervous at first, scared that I might say or do the wrong thing, but quickly realized I had nothing to worry about. They talked nonstop all the way to my apartment. They told me everything I needed to know about the club, including the fact that Henley was married to Maverick, the club's Sergeant at Arms, and all about how Cassidy ended up being the president's old lady. They took their time explaining each of the officers – from Guardrail, the VP, and Allie, to Clutch, the road captain, and his girl Olivia. Knowing Tristen had a thing for him, I paid close attention when they talked about Smokey and MJ. Both Cassidy and Henley seemed to think a lot of him, making me think he wasn't the bad guy I'd like to think he was. Actually, they all seemed like good guys. By the time they were finished, I knew about all the brothers and what role they played. They even told me a little more about Big. While it was a lot to take in, I was glad they shared it with me.

As soon as Cassidy pulled up to my apartment, I hopped out of the car and rushed up the stairs. I pulled the keys out of my pocket and unlocked the door. I motioned for them to come inside. "This is it."

"It's so freaking cute!" Henley squealed. Thomas was propped on her hip and looked absolutely adorable with his dark hair and beautiful green eyes. He babbled and cooed as his mother carried him through my kitchen and into the living room.

"Thanks." It was small, but I'd done what I could to spruce it up the best I could. I'd learned a thing or two about decoupage, and I'd redone several pieces of junked-out furniture and made them look new. I'd also put a fresh coat of grey paint in the living room and my bedroom, and I'd hung several of my oversized black and white photographs on the walls. Some would call it eclectic with all the mismatched pieces of furniture and bright colors, but it was mine and I liked it.

Cassidy ran her hand across the top of my sofa table and smiled. "Did you make this?"

"Not exactly." I grabbed my duffle bag out of the side closet and started towards my bedroom. "I bought it at a yard sale a few years back and refinished it."

"It's awesome. I just love the color. I wish I could do stuff like this."

"It's not hard. Just find a piece you like and I'll show you how to do it."

"Really?" she asked, sounding surprised.

"Of course." I went into my room and shoved several pairs of jeans and some t-shirts into my bag. Then I grabbed my makeup bag and a few other necessities. I was just about to call it a day when my favorite outfit caught my eye. I quickly reached for it and put it in my bag with the rest of my things. When I came out of my room, I found Cass and Henley talking softly in the corner. I stepped closer and realized they were looking at a picture I had of me and Tristen when we were kids. It was one of my favorite pictures of us. We'd been swimming in our neighbor's pool, and we had our beach towels wrapped tightly around our waists and big smiles plastered on our faces. It was a time when we were truly happy, long before we lost our parents. I cleared my throat to let them know I was behind them and said, "All set."

There was a sadness in Cassidy's eyes. "I haven't really had the chance to tell you how sorry we are about Tristen. It's hard to believe any of this is happening."

"Trust me, I know." I sighed.

Henley walked over to me and placed her hand on my arm. "We're all praying that she'll be okay."

"Thanks, Henley." I swallowed hard, trying my best to keep my tears at bay. "Every time we'd talk, Tristen would have some wild story to tell me about the club. She'd laugh and carry on, and it was obvious that she was happy there. I never understood it. I always thought she was just going through another phase or she was still trying to rebel… but after being there myself and getting the chance to know you all, I finally get it."

Henley smiled. "I'm glad to hear that. We like having you around."

Cassidy added, "And Tristen would be tickled to

hear you say that. She was worried about disappointing you."

"Disappointing me? She could never disappoint me." I thought back to our last few conversations, remembering how she made sure to tell me about all the things she was doing with her new job and the nice people she was working with. It never dawned on me that she was hoping to gain my approval. I was too busy worrying that I'd say the wrong thing, thinking one wrong slip and I might lose her, so she never knew how proud I was of her. I should've told her. I should've made it clear that there was nothing she could do that would make me love her any less. "She's my sister. As long as she's happy, then I'm happy."

"That's what I told her." Cassidy smiled. "And when we get her back, you can tell her yourself."

Thomas started to fuss, so Henley said, "Time to get this little guy some lunch. Are you guys ready to head back?"

"Yep. I'm good to go."

After I locked everything up, I followed them down to the car and we headed back to the clubhouse. While they went to the kitchen to feed Thomas, I went back to Tristen's room to drop off my bag. When I walked in, I was surprised to find a new laptop sitting on her desk. I stepped closer and spotted an envelope with my name on it sitting on top. I quickly opened it and found a short note from Big.

Josie,

Might want to avoid drinking soda when using this one.

Big

I laughed out loud when I read it. I could only imagine the mess I'd made when I poured my drink over my computer. By now, I'm sure it was a sugary, corroded mess, so I was thankful Big had gotten me a new one. I eagerly turned it on and was thrilled to see all my favorite programs were already installed, and he'd included the files that he was able to retrieve from my old laptop. I had just assumed that Big had tossed all my old files when he'd scrubbed my computer. I had no idea why he'd gone to all the trouble, but couldn't have been more excited. Feeling the need to express my gratitude, I decided to go see Big.

As soon as I knocked, he shouted, "It's open."

When I opened the door, I found him sitting at his desk. "Hey."

"Hey, yourself." He motioned me over to him. "Come on in."

I couldn't stop myself from staring as I walked over and sat down beside him. He was wearing a dark, long-sleeved t-shirt and a pair of faded jeans. The man was fully clothed. It should've helped, but it didn't—not even a little. I was still gawking at him like some sex-crazed teenager. Eventually, I forced my eyes up towards his face and away from the snug, fitted t-shirt and the rippling muscles of his chest. When I finally managed to make eye contact with him, I found him smirking at me. My ogling hadn't gone unnoticed. Damn. "I… uhh… I wanted to thank you for the new laptop."

His smile quickly faded. "Figured you'd need it when we get to LA."

"LA?"

"We'll be heading there tomorrow to get Tristen."

"Why do I feel like I'm missing some key information?"

He sighed as he turned his body towards me. "Nitro has a plan to get your sister back. It's risky, but I think it'll work."

"He knows where she is?"

"He does."

"You going to tell me or do I have to keep imagining the worst?"

"What you're imagining can't be much worse." He continued to explain everything that Nitro had told him, and by the time he'd finished telling me everything, I was a complete mess. He was right; I couldn't have imagined anything so horrific. My precious sister was caught up in a sex-trafficking ring, and if they weren't able to get her back, she'd be lost to me forever. Panic started to set in as I stood up and started pacing back and forth across the room. I was about to have a total breakdown when I felt Big's arms wrap around me. He pulled me close, holding me tightly as he whispered, "You're not in this alone. I'm right here with you, Josie."

Despite the overwhelming dread churning in my stomach, I felt a sense of comfort when my body pressed against his. Since my parents died, I learned to do things on my own. I didn't have a choice. I had relatives, people who cared about me, but they always assumed I had it all figured out. They just assumed my parents had taken care of everything for me, but they were wrong. They'd left me money, plenty of money, but that was about it. I enrolled myself into college and managed to find a decent apartment. I got a job, maintained my grades, and never missed a class. I became independent because I had to, but now, for the first time in a long time, I had someone to lean on: Big. I sunk into the warmth of his side, relishing in the calming sensation of his touch. Just being close to him gave me hope, making the future seem a little less bleak. "Thank you. I don't think I could make it through all this without you."

His arms squeezed a fraction tighter, and I started to breathe a little easier. "I know it isn't easy. None of this is easy, but you've gotta find a way to keep it together."

"I'm trying." I held onto him, not wanting the moment to end. "When will we be leaving?"

He took a step back and reached for an envelope off

Big

his desk. He handed it to me. "We'll head out tomorrow night. That will give us forty-eight hours to get everything set up."

I looked down at the tickets, seeing that we had a direct flight into Los Angeles leaving at seven the following evening. My chest tightened when I noticed there were three tickets, not two. Before I could ask, he took a step towards me. "Stitch."

"Seriously? Out of all the guys you've got around here, he's the one that's gotta come?"

"He's the enforcer for a reason."

Even if he was the freaking terminator, it was still just the four of us going up against the Mexican cartel alone. "How are we going to pull this off, Big?"

"Nitro's already got his seat at the table. His guy told them he was looking for some new arm candy."

"Nitro isn't the kind of man who needs to pay for arm candy."

Big chuckled under his breath. "No, he's not, but they don't know that. For all they know, he's a busy man with no time on his hands. Easier for him to just buy some hot piece of ass. Doll her up and use her anyway he pleases."

"That's awful."

"Those are the good guys, Josie. Some of these guys are real sickos. They'll do unimaginable things to these women and think nothing of it."

"What if one of those men try to buy…"

"That won't happen. Nitro will out bid anyone who

tries to buy her."

Realizing that he hadn't explained my part in all of this, I asked, "What exactly do you need *me* to do?"

"Once we get the location, we're going to try to tap into their security feed. If we're able to pull it off, you'll be able to monitor everything that happens while we're inside. I'll have a two-way radio headset for us to communicate back and forth."

"You think they will let you inside with that?"

He opened his desk drawer and pulled out a tiny clear earpiece. "They'll never see it. With the camera footage, we will be able to see where their guards are posted, and you can give us a heads-up if there are any surprises."

"And where exactly will I be when I'm doing all this monitoring?"

"At the hotel."

He seemed to have all the answers, where I was left with an endless amount of questions. "So, you already know where we'll be staying?"

"Not yet. Nitro is handling that."

"What about…" I started, but stopped myself. I was driving myself batty, so I could only imagine how crazy I was making Big.

"Get some rest. You're going to need it."

B*Big* Chapter 11

When I'd told myself that I was going to keep my distance, that I was going to fight the pull I'd been feeling towards Josie, I didn't realize just how hard it was going to be. I kept finding myself thinking and worrying about her. Even though she tried to keep up a brave front, I knew she was having a rough go of it. Hell, she'd already lost her parents, and now this shit with her sister. Just the thought of having someone that I cared about taken by the cartel was enough to make my blood run cold. She'd put all her trust in us, knowing we were her only hope, but there was always that haunting fear that we'd fail, leaving her sister in a horrific situation. For anyone else, the thought would be soul crushing, but Josie was still standing strong. She was determined and wouldn't give up until we brought Tristen home. When she left my room, I'd hoped that she'd spend the day preparing herself for the trip ahead, and maybe even take some time to relax before all the hell began. Unfortunately, she wasn't taking that much needed break. Instead, I found her in the bar staring at her laptop, and from the look on her face, it was clear that she was troubled by what was on that screen.

She didn't even notice when I walked up. I looked over her shoulder, and when I noticed what she was reading, I asked, "Why are you doing this to yourself?"

Her eyes never left the screen as she answered, "I had to see for myself."

I had no idea what all she'd read, but I knew it wasn't good. The pictures alone were enough to make my stomach turn. "I don't think that's a good idea."

"Did you know most of these women are actually sold by their own families? Some of them don't know what's really happening. They think they're doing something to help their child escape poverty or to get them into the States, but there are others that know exactly what they're doing."

"It's fucked up."

"It is. I can't imagine doing that to someone I cared about."

Her voice cracked, letting me know it was time for her little study session to end. It might've been a mistake, but it was clear she needed a friend. "Let's go."

She looked up at me with confusion. "Go where?"

"Gonna take a ride."

"I don't…"

I cut her off. "It's not up for discussion."

"Umm… okay." She closed her laptop and stood up from the table. "Let me grab a jacket."

"I'll meet you out front in the parking lot," I told her as I started for the door. I went out to my bike, and I'd just gotten my helmet on when she stepped outside. Just the sight of her walking towards me took my breath away. She was wearing a fitted, black leather jacket and a pair of dark jeans with boots, and her long, wavy hair fell loose around her shoulders. Pure perfection. Once she made her way over to me, she pulled her hair to the side and slipped on her helmet. "You ready?"

"Always." I waited for her to get on and settle behind me before I started the engine. With no real destination in mind, I pulled out of the gate and onto the highway. I thought taking a ride might help Josie clear her head. I wasn't thinking how much good it would do me, too. As soon as that wind hit my face, it was as if all the cares and concerns of the day, the week, and all that was going on released its grip on me. The roar of the engine and the clean, crisp air rushing by my ears was like a powerful symphony playing music directly into my soul. Add the fact that Josie was behind me, her arms tightly wrapped around my waist, and my day couldn't have been better.

We'd been riding for almost an hour when I found myself pulling into Smokey's place. I figured Josie might need a break, and the orchard was the perfect place to stretch our legs. When I pulled around to the back and killed the engine, Josie asked, "An apple orchard? What made you think to come here?"

"It's Smokey's place. Thought we'd take a look around."

She got off the bike and took her helmet off as she looked over at the barn. "It's beautiful."

"They've done some work on the place. Smokey just had the house remodeled, and I think they're planning to expand the barn at some point."

"Smokey is one of the brothers, right?"

"He is."

"And he runs an *apple orchard*?"

"It's complicated," I told her as I took off my helmet. Smokey inherited the place when his father died. He was reluctant to take it on, but with MJ's help, he decided to give it a go. Together, they'd managed to make it a success again. We walked past the barn and out into the orchard where we found rows upon rows of apple trees. Harvest season was still months away, but the trees were beautiful. I looked at Josie and was relieved to see that she seemed better. Relaxed, even. We continued to stroll along the dirt path, enjoying the warmth of the sun on our backs and the cool breeze on our faces while we left our worries of the upcoming days behind us.

"So, do all the brothers have jobs outside of the club?"

Club business was off-limits. It wasn't discussed with anyone, especially with someone outside the club, so I left it simple. "Guardrail runs our construction company. Most of the guys work out there with him while some of us do some odds and ends in the garage."

"And Guardrail is the VP of the club?"

"He is."

A mischievous grin crossed her face as she asked, "What about you? Do you have a special role or an official position?"

"I fill in wherever they need me."

"Mmm-hmm." She continued to walk as she shook her head playfully. "Don't know many garages that need themselves a computer hacker, Big."

"*Josie*," I warned.

"I know, I know. Certain questions shouldn't be asked, but I thought I'd give it a shot."

She was smiling. Nothing else mattered in that moment. We continued to talk as we started back towards the barn. When we made it to the bike, Smokey was there waiting on us. "You should've told me you were coming. I'd have given you the full tour."

"It's trees, Smokey. I think we managed just fine without a guide."

"You must be Josie," Smokey said as he extended his hand to her. "Heard a lot about you."

"I could say the same about you."

Smokey looked over at me with a shit-eating grin as he snickered. "Maybe, but my stories aren't as cool as yours. Heard about you pulling a fast one on Big."

Damn. They weren't ever gonna let it go. Choosing to change the subject before it even got started, I asked, "Where's MJ?"

"She's at the office. Had some big case come in. Been at it for over a week now."

"We'll catch her next time."

I handed Josie her helmet and got on the bike. Before she had a chance to join me, Smokey turned to her and said, "I'm sorry to hear about all this mess with

Tristen."

At just the mention of her name, Josie's entire demeanor changed. Her body grew tense and that smile she'd been wearing quickly faded. The carefree sparkle in her eye all but disappeared as she replied, "Thanks, Smokey. I'm hoping it will all be over soon."

"Big's the best. I'd trust him with my life. If anyone can bring her back, it'll be him."

"Let's hope you're right." She smiled and climbed on the bike behind me. "It was nice to meet you, Smokey."

"Same here. You two be careful out there."

"Will do, brother. See ya back at the clubhouse. Church is at seven."

"I'll be there."

I started the engine and headed down the long gravel driveway. I didn't waste any time getting back to the clubhouse. The sun had just started to set, and the temperature was falling fast. By the time we made it back, Josie's cheeks were bright pink and her teeth were chattering. She followed me inside and over to the bar. Cassidy came over and asked, "What can I get ya?"

"Two shots of bourbon and a couple of beers."

"You got it." Seconds later, she brought our drinks over and set them down on the counter. "You two have a nice ride?"

"We did." Josie smiled. "Big took me out to Smokey's orchard."

"Oh, it's so pretty out there. I could spend the

Big

whole day just walking around."

"I loved the barn, and the house was beautiful."

"You should see inside. Smokey completely redid the place." Some of the guys walked in and sat down at the other end of the bar. "Gotta run. Let me know if you need anything else."

Josie looked at me and smiled. "I really like her."

"She's a good one." I'd already taken my shot while Josie's remained untouched on the counter. "You gonna drink that, or wait 'til someone else snatches it up?"

She took the shot glass in her hand and quickly downed it. Her nose crinkled as the alcohol burned its way down her throat. "Damn. That's awful."

"Yeah, but it'll warm you up."

"Or burn right through me." She reached for her beer and took a long drink before placing it back on the counter.

"Did you enjoy the ride?"

"I loved it. Thanks so much for taking me, Big. You saved me from myself. All that reading was freaking me out."

"Glad I could help. You had me worried there for a minute."

"No more online searching."

I nodded. "That'd probably be for the best."

She sighed as she said, "I guess I better go pack."

"You got a dress or something nice to wear?"

A curious look crossed her face as she looked over

to me. "Why?"

"You might need it."

"I'm sure I can come up with something." After taking one more drink of her beer, she stood up and turned to me with a smile. "I really did have fun today."

"I did, too." More than she knew.

By the time I'd finished my beer, it was time for church. Cotton had already informed the brothers about Tristen's kidnapping, and he'd called us all together to discuss our plan for bringing her home. Once we were settled, Cotton shared every detail of our plan with the brothers, and I could see that they were concerned. It was risky. We all knew that, but with Nitro's help, I had to believe we'd pull it off.

As soon as we were dismissed, Cotton came over to me and placed his hand on my shoulder. "You all set?"

"Getting there."

"If you need anything, you just let me know."

"Will do, Prez."

"Don't go playing the hero." His grip tightened on my shoulder. "I want you to get her out of there, but don't get yourself killed doing it."

"You got it."

"I'm holding you to that shit, Mike. We need you around here. Don't want to lose you." He gave my shoulder a quick slap before he turned to leave. As I followed him out, I prayed that I'd be able to keep my word.

Chapter 12
Josie

My heart was hammering against my chest as we headed towards the front door of the airport. I tried to keep my pace casual with no hint of hesitation, but it was damn near impossible. I felt like every nerve in my body was set on high, making it difficult to even function. I wanted them to think I was feeling confident, that my mind wasn't teetering on the edge of a mental breakdown, so I tried to appear nonchalant, praying that my flushed cheeks and fidgeting fingers wouldn't betray me. I didn't want to give the guys any reason to doubt their decision to bring me along. I wanted to be there, wanted to help bring my sister home, but that didn't stop the fear from coursing through my veins. I knew what we were planning to do was dangerous, I knew there was a chance we would fail, and it terrified me to think Tristen might not make it back home. There were so many unanswered questions, questions that I was too afraid to ask. I didn't want to think about it—the thought of losing my sister was just too much to bear. I tried to fight it, but my mind was bombarded with doubts as we continued towards our terminal. Each step brought on more anxiety, more terrifying thoughts, and the fact that neither Big nor Stitch spoke a single word wasn't helping. I could almost feel the tension rolling off them as we made our way to the gate. Thankfully, by the time we met up with Nitro and two of his men at our gate, they were already calling us to board the plane.

Big placed the palm of his hand on the small of my back and guided me up to the attendant. I handed her my ticket and carefully walked onto the boarding bridge. Once I stepped inside the plane, I went to find my seat. I found it with no problem and sat down. I'd barely gotten settled when Stitch plopped down next to me. I looked around the plane, and Big was nowhere in sight. When I turned back in my seat, Stitch was staring right at me. Damn.

"He's a few rows in front of us."

"Umm… *okay*." I looked out the window and stared out into the dark, trying to pretend that it wasn't bugging the hell out of me that the man who had tortured me for hours was sitting right beside me. It wasn't fear, but anger I felt when I looked at him. I knew it wasn't his fault and he was just doing his job, but that didn't change the fact that he'd hurt me. I found myself thinking of little ways I could seek my revenge—like a hard jab into his side with my elbow or pouring hot coffee on his crotch or, even better yet, shaving off his precious beard. I was still conjuring up ideas when the attendant came by to offer us a beverage. Stitch had his head leaned back against his seat and his eyes were closed. I reached for my drink, feeling the cold bite of the ice against my hand, and a smile spread across my face when I thought about dumping it in

Big

Stitch's lap.

He cracked one eye open and glared at me. "Don't even think about it."

"What?" I asked defensively.

"You know what." He closed his eyes once again and feigned sleep. Asshole.

I wanted to forget it ever happened, but every time I looked at him, the memories came trudging back— every surge of pain that jolted through my body when he electrocuted me, the burning sensations that tingled throughout my hands and feet, the taste of copper in my mouth when I bit my tongue. I'd tried to stay strong, thinking I was doing what I had to do to save Tristen, and I'd do it all over again if I thought it would bring her back. Unfortunately, no amount of pain he inflicted on me was going to bring her back.

"You're not going to let it go, are you?" he asked with his eyebrow cocked.

"What? The fact that you nearly froze me to death and then electrocuted me, like, twenty times? No, I've let all that go a long time ago."

A shiver rippled down my spine as he turned in his seat to face me. The serious look on his face made me regret provoking him. "First, it was three times, not twenty, and I was taking it easy on you."

"Easy on me? Nothing about that was easy."

"You know why I had to do it."

In my mind, I understood. It was my heart that was having the problem letting go. No one had ever hurt me

117

like that, and I was having a hard time forgiving him. His bossy attitude wasn't helping matters. "Maybe so, but that doesn't make it right."

"You gotta remember one thing, Josie. You might not like it, you might not understand it, but at the end of the day, I do whatever it takes to protect my family. *Nothing* stops me."

I remember Big saying something similar. Stitch was the enforcer for a reason, but hearing it straight from the horse's mouth sent chills down my spine. I'd seen for myself what he could do, and I had no doubt that he meant it when he said he took it easy on me. I didn't know what the next forty-eight hours would bring, but I found myself feeling relieved that Stitch was on my side helping us get my sister back, because I had a feeling we were going to need a man like him to bring her home. While it was still there and gnawing at me, I felt the panic start to dwindle. Maybe, just maybe, we'd be able to pull this thing off. "You know… you're a real charmer."

His lips twitched into a grin. "That's what I've been told."

It was the first time I'd actually seen the man smile, and I hated to admit it, but it looked good on him. His whole demeanor changed, showing that there was another side to him. I liked the smile. I actually found comfort in it and wanted to keep it there. "By the way, your daughter is beautiful."

I'd found his soft spot, and at just the mention of

her, his face lit up. "She is. Looks like her mother."

"Are you two planning on having any more kids?"

The stiffness in his back eased as he leaned back in his chair. "Maybe someday. We're still trying to manage the two."

"Yeah, Wren seemed pretty upset about Wyatt's teacher the other day. Did she get everything worked out?"

The tension in his body returned, letting me know I'd just screwed the pooch by bringing it up. "What about Wyatt's teacher?"

I tried to blow it off. "I'm sure it was nothing. She was just a little flustered. No big deal."

"*Josie.*"

"Honestly, I don't remember much about it. It was the first time I'd met everyone, and my mind was still pretty much fried from my night from hell." He just sat there staring at me, so I knew he wasn't going to let it go. "She mentioned you weren't in a good mood, and Wyatt's teacher was giving him a hard time. She was worried about him and you."

"Fuck."

"I'm sorry. I shouldn't have said anything. I wasn't thinking."

"No. It's on me, not you." He rolled his head back and forth, trying to ease the tension in his neck. "I should've known something was up."

"It's been a hectic few days. I'm sure she understands." Seeing Stitch in his husband-slash-father role was an interesting sight to see. There are plenty of men in the world who wouldn't have cared, so it meant something that he was so concerned and that he wanted to know what was going on with his son. I probably should've left it, but I asked, "Wren mentioned that he was... *different*. Do you mind me asking what she meant?"

"He has a high-functioning form of Asperger's. Honestly, I don't see anything all that different about him other than he's smart as hell. He's an amazing kid."

"He's lucky to have a dad who thinks that way."

"It's the truth. All of us are different in our own way. I'd take his kind of different any day."

"Can I offer one piece of advice?" I smiled.

"Yeah?"

"If you go with Wren to talk to his knucklehead teacher, leave your Taser thingie at home."

His body shook with laughter. "Yeah, you're probably right about that."

"Hopefully she will figure out what a great kid Wyatt is on her own. Sometimes, it just takes a little time."

"Maybe so."

The seatbelt sign lit up, letting us know the plane was about to land. Fear surged through me when I realized we were about to be in the same city where my sister was being held captive. There was so much going against us, and the chance of getting my sister back was slim, to say the least. I just prayed that these men knew what the hell they were doing and we didn't all get ourselves killed. Stitch must've picked up on my apprehension, so he placed his hand on my arm. "It'll be all right, Josie. One way or another, we are bringing Tristen back."

There was no doubt resting behind his eyes – only pure determination. "Thank you."

"No need to thank me. Just doing my job."

The plane landed, and after we grabbed our bags, we went straight to our rental car. Big had gotten us a black SUV with dark tinted windows. After we put our bags into the back, Big walked over and got in the driver's seat while Nitro got in beside him. Nitro's guys crawled into the very back of the vehicle, leaving Stitch and me to sit together in the middle. This time I didn't feel the same apprehension as I did earlier. Surprisingly, I'd let go of my resentment for him and was actually starting to like the man. I'd been so wrong about so many things, especially my attitude towards the men of Satan's Fury. They may in fact do bad things, but they are good men with hearts that bleed and souls that are pure and true. They are loyal to a fault, and I would forever be indebted to them for helping me.

We pulled up to the hotel and my mouth dropped open. The place looked like something out of a movie. It must've cost a fortune to get a room here, a place for politicians, doctors, and lawyers, and I wondered how Nitro could afford it. I had the sneaking suspicion that his money hadn't come from a legitimate occupation, making me wonder what he actually did to make his fortune. "We're staying here?"

"Yep," Nitro answered.

"It's beautiful, but …"

Big turned to me and said, "Gotta keep up the show. Nitro is supposed to be a high roller. It's expected that he'll stay in the best place in town."

"Supposed to be? Hell, I am," Nitro snickered. "Highest mother fucking roller around."

"And that's why you eat ramen noodles most nights," Big taunted.

"No. I eat ramen noodles because they are the shit, brother. Pop those suckers in the microwave, and a minute later, you have yourself a hot meal."

"You need yourself a woman."

Nitro's brows furrowed and his lips dropped into a frown. "I need a woman like I need a fucking bullet to the head."

"Just saying… there's something to be said for coming home to a hot meal on the table." Stitch smiled as he waited for Nitro to respond.

"I'll settle for a hot piece of ass any day."

Listening to their banter made me realize why women don't travel alone with three men. I think they'd all but forgotten that I was still sitting there, so I added, "The trick is finding someone who will give you both."

I kept my smile to myself when they all turned and looked at me with surprise. Choosing to end the conversation there, Big parked the truck and we all got out. I did my best to act unfazed as we walked into the fancy hotel. It was like walking into another world and hiding my apprehension wasn't easy. Everything glittered and shined, including all the people who stopped in their tracks and watched as we approached the front desk. The beautiful blonde receptionist smiled as she asked, "How may I help you tonight?"

"Checking in. Nathan James."

After a few clicks on her keyboard, her eyes widened with disbelief. She quickly collected herself and purred, "Yes, Mr. James. We have the penthouse suite ready for you, along with two other rooms."

He took out his credit card and slid it across the counter in her direction. "That'll be perfect."

After she rang everything up, she looked up at Nitro. Her long eyelashes fluttered as she leaned towards him and licked her bottom lip as she offered him the electronic room cards. "You're all set. Is there anything else I can help you with, Mr. James?"

There's friendly, and then there's the "I'm a whore, come screw me later tonight" kind of friendly. This chick was the latter, and Nitro seemed amused by her advances. A mischievous grin crossed his face as he took the cards from her hand. "This will do it… *for now*."

"I'll be right here if you need anything *at all*."

After a quick nod, he turned and started for the elevator. No one spoke as we made it up to the top floor. Once we reached the penthouse, Nitro placed the card in the slot and the door clicked open. We followed him inside and I marveled at how big and luxurious the room was. I found myself staring at Nitro with visions of bank heists and large crates of drugs crossing the border. When the men started talking amongst themselves, I started to meander through the room, running the tips of my fingers across the soft fabrics and the cold marble countertops, and I was amazed at how spectacular everything was. I'd always wondered what these rooms were like, but I could've never imagined they'd be like this. I was still lost in wonder when Big walked over to me. "You ready to get settled?"

"Sure."

Big took a few steps and opened the door to the side suite revealing an additional bedroom. "I'll bring your bags up in a bit."

"Wait. I'm staying up here… with Nitro?"

"Yes."

"But why?"

"Like you said, Nitro isn't the kind of man who has to pay for arm candy."

"Seriously? I'm supposed to be with him?"

"It's just for show, Josie. He'll stay in his room, and his guys will crash on the sofas. Consider it a small sacrifice to get your sister back."

I fought the frantic frenzy that was building inside of me, knowing I would do anything to help them find Tristen. Even though I wasn't thrilled with the arrangement, I accepted my fate and stepped inside the room. "Fine."

I was about to shut the door when I felt Big's hand on my arm and I was suddenly pulled back over to him. His eyes locked on mine with a fierceness that demanded my attention. "Just so you know, I don't like this any more than you do. If I had it my way, you'd be in my room… in *my* bed."

His words hit me like a two-ton truck. I knew there was an attraction between us, I'd felt it since he'd pulled me down from that hook, but he'd never acted on it. Before I had a chance to react, he released his hold on my arm and walked away, leaving me standing there in a complete daze. Damn. I couldn't tell if I was coming or going as I closed the door and walked over to the bed. I didn't even bother changing clothes before crawling under the covers. There were so many emotions swirling inside of me, making me just want to curl up into a ball and cry. Tristen was just a few miles away. I wanted to go to her, tear her away from those monsters, and run far, far away from this place. Without even realizing I was crying, I felt my tears trickling down my cheeks. I'd tried so hard, did everything I could think of to get to her, and the fear of messing things up scared me to death. One wrong move and everything I'd tried to do would be in vain. I'd just about worked myself into a complete meltdown when I heard a tap at my door. I quickly wiped my tears from my face and sat up on the bed.

"It's open."

Nitro stepped inside with my duffle bag in his hand. "Big just dropped this off."

"Thanks. Just leave it by the door."

With his voice filled with concern, he asked, "You doing okay?"

"Yeah. I'm fine. Just tired."

"I could order some room service or something?"

It was sweet of him to offer, but I wasn't in the mood for food or company. "I'm good. Just need to get some sleep."

"Suit yourself." He turned to leave, but before he left, he turned back to me and said, "It's okay to be scared. It's okay to have a complete meltdown and trudge through the damn swamps. Do what you gotta do, but by morning, you're gonna have to shake that shit off. We need you, and your sister does, too."

Chapter 13

After spending the entire night with no sleep, I was irritable and on edge, and to make matters worse, my bad night was rolling over into a bad afternoon. I'd spent the early morning hours trying to get everything ready for the following night, and my list of things to do was steadily growing. I was busting my ass to pull it all together while my buddy Nitro was having himself a relaxing afternoon by the fucking pool.

I walked over to his lounge chair and growled, "Stitch and I are ready to set up. Gonna need the location."

Nitro took a drag off his cigarette. "What's with the mood? It's a beautiful day."

"*Nitro.*"

"Should have it sometime tomorrow evening."

Everything depended on us hacking into their security feed. Without it, we'd have to go in blind, leaving us no idea what the hell we were up against. "This shit takes time. We need it now."

"They won't give the exact location until a couple of hours before the auction. Nothing new there, brother."

"And you didn't think to mention that shit?"

"Figured it wouldn't take you long to get in there

and get what you needed, especially with *her* helping ya." His head motioned over to the back gate.

All the blood rushed to my cock when I spotted Josie walking in our direction. She was wearing a tiny black bikini and dark sunglasses. Her hair was pulled up into some fancy braid, and she was wearing big silver hoop earrings with silver bangles dangling at her wrists. *Damn.* She looked like something out of the *Sports Illustrated* swimsuit edition as she lowered herself onto the lounge chair and leaned her head back. "Afternoon, boys."

"Looking good, sweetheart." Nitro winked at her, and it took every ounce of my restraint not to slam my fist into his throat.

"Thanks, pumpkin," Josie purred.

I couldn't believe what I was hearing. "You wanna tell me what the hell you think you're doing?"

"What?" She shrugged and cocked her eyebrow. "It's all just for show, Big. You know… just a *small sacrifice* to get my sister back."

After throwing my own words back in my face, she took one of the magazines off the side table and pretended to read it. Damn it all to hell. The woman was going to drive me over the fucking edge and make me do something we'd all regret.

I decided not to rile up Josie any more than she already was, so I turned my attention to Nitro when he spoke. "We've got company coming."

I'd learned a long time ago that Nitro answered to

no one. He ran things his way – and only *his* way – but now was not a time for him to keep me in the dark, especially with Josie being involved. "What kind of company?"

His eyes skirted over to Josie before he answered. "Just a *friend* looking to discuss a business opportunity. I have no interest in starting up anything with this guy, so it shouldn't take long."

"And Josie needs to be here for this shit? Dressed like that?"

She pulled her sunglasses down to the tip of her nose and glared at me. "It's a bikini, Big. It's not like I'm getting ready to slide down a stripper pole or anything."

As soon as the words left her mouth, visions of her twirling around in that fucking bikini and a pair of high heels came crashing through my mind. I had to stop thinking with my dick and focus. "And this friend of yours... is he someone I should be concerned about?"

His eyes widened as he cocked his neck to the side, letting me know he didn't want Josie to know there was trouble coming. "Business as usual. Why don't you grab yourself a drink and take a load off?"

I took a quick glance around the pool, looking for anything suspicious, and spotted Stitch sitting across from us. He was leaning back in his chair as he sat under an umbrella with his jeans and a white t-shirt. I'd love to say that he was blending in and no one had even seen him sitting there, but a group of women were eyeballing him from across the pool. I was about to walk over to him when I spotted four men scattered along the edge of the balcony. "Aren't those your guys?"

Nitro looked up. "Yeah. Got two more around back."

"That's six, Nitro. You only brought two."

"Called the others in when *my friend* requested a meet." His voice was stern and almost reprimanding. I knew he was trying to get me to drop it, but he always left out information I needed to know. I felt certain this time was no different.

"I'm gonna go get that drink," I told him as I started walking towards the bar. After ordering a glass of ice water, I sat down at one of the tables under the canopy and waited. It didn't take long for Nitro's guests to arrive. They strolled in wearing short-sleeved dress shirts, revealing all their ink and gangster-style hats. The ring leader walked in front while his thugs strolled behind him checking out all the chicks at the pool.

Nitro slowly stood from his chair and greeted his so-called friend. They bantered back and forth for several minutes, and then the guy turned his attention to Josie. The way he looked at her, like she was a fucking piece of meat, made me come out of my skin. Thankfully, their conversation ended quickly and the men turned and left. Before Nitro had a chance to sit down, I whistled and motioned him over to the bar.

Now that we were alone, I asked, "What the hell

was that?"

"That was me ensuring that things will go our way tomorrow night," he smirked. "The guy? That was Pacheco."

"Who the fuck is Pacheco?"

"The boss's right-hand man." He ran his fingers through his hair and sighed. "My guy got to bragging. Wanted me to come off as a big player. He was sent to make sure I was legit."

"You think he bought it?"

A smug look crossed his face as he answered, "Absolutely. Why wouldn't he? I *am* a big player, brother. Hell, the guy even wanted to know what kind of girl I was looking for. All but guaranteed I'd have whatever I wanted."

"Well, at least there's that."

"It's all set. So now we just wait."

When Nitro started walking back towards Josie, I growled, "Tell her she can wait *inside* and to put some damned clothes on."

He looked back over his shoulder and snickered, "Nope. I'm enjoying the view way too much for that, brother."

Choosing to swallow my rage, I stormed out of the bar. I had no right to be angry. Josie was just doing what she'd been asked to do, and I was being an overprotective, jealous asshole. I couldn't help myself. Every time I laid eyes on her, my entire body ached. I wanted Josie to be mine, and not having her was fucking with my head. Once I got back to the room, I went straight for the bathroom. I needed a cold shower followed by several stiff drinks. It was the only way I was going to shake the unwanted feelings that were burning in the pit of my stomach.

I don't know how long I stayed in that shower, but it wasn't long enough. I got out with the same feeling of hunger and one hell of a hard-on. I reached for my boxers and groaned out loud when my dick pitched a tent beneath the fabric. I was considering another cold shower when I heard a knock at my door. I should've checked to see who it was so I could've prepared myself, but my aggravation with my dick made me lose focus. Without reaching for my pants, or my shirt, or even a fucking towel, I yelled, "It's open."

The door eased open and my breath stopped as Josie stepped inside. She was still wearing that damned bikini, and my tent got three inches taller. Fuck. Thankfully, she was too pissed to notice. "What the hell was that at the pool?"

"If you don't know, then there's no point in saying it."

She threw her hands up in the air with aggravation. "What's that supposed to mean?"

"It's nothing."

A scowl crossed her face as she took another step towards me. "Don't you give me that bullshit. You're the one who asked me to play hooker for Nitro, and then you have the audacity to get mad at me about it."

"I'm not mad."

"Seriously? You're gonna try to blow off that little display?"

"You need to remember that not everything is about you, Josie."

I could see from the grimace on her face that my words stung, but they didn't stop her from coming at me again. Without hesitating, she snapped, "Oh, no! This has nothing to do with me. This is about you."

"Oh, yeah? What about *me*?" I crossed my arms and waited for her to continue.

She looked at me with defeat and said, "God, just forget it."

Regret washed over me as I watched her turn towards the door. I should have let her walk out that door. Nothing good would come from having her stay, but the thought of her leaving made me call out to her. "Josie… wait."

"*What?*" she pleaded as she spun around. "Just tell me what is *really* going on with you! Your words tell me one thing, Michael Davis, but your eyes…" she continued as she took another step towards me, "say something else entirely. For once, just tell me what you're really thinking."

Hearing the sound of my name from her lips was the ultimate seduction. I wanted her. There was no denying that, but I knew having her came at a cost. "Not sure I can do that."

She walked over to me and gently placed the palm

of her hand against my chest. "Tell me."

I didn't have the words to tell her, so I showed her. I took a step towards her and placed my hand on the nape of her neck, pulling her mouth to mine. The touch of her lips set me on fire, and I knew there was no going back, no more keeping my restraint. I would have this moment with her, and to hell with the consequences. I'd never felt such a hunger for a woman, and from the way she kissed me, there was no doubt she felt the same. It felt like I'd waited a lifetime to feel her in my arms, and now that I'd finally had her, I was afraid I'd never be able to let her go. She felt too good, too right. The scent of her skin and the warmth of her mouth seduced my senses, making me want her even more. My hands made their way past the small of her back down to her perfect ass where I pulled her close against my body. A soft whimper escaped from her lips as they parted, allowing me to kiss her deeper. Her arms wound around my neck as I guided her over towards the bed and slowly lowered her down onto the mattress. She was absolutely divine, and I wanted to explore every inch. I trailed kisses down her neck, causing goosebumps to prickle against her skin as I made my way to her collarbone, then to her breasts.

I slipped my hands behind her back, gently releasing the clasp of her bikini top, and lowered it down her shoulders, revealing her perfect round breasts. I was in absolute heaven as I dropped my mouth to her nipple, sucking and nipping at her sensitive flesh. She

Big

was so damned perfect—just like I knew she'd be. Her heart, her body, everything called out to me, like she was made for me. She threw her head back and arched her back up towards my mouth as moans echoed around us. I looked up at her, seeing the effect that I was having on her, and my cock throbbed against my boxers. My mouth never left her breast as I drug my hard shaft against her center.

"Yes!" she chanted over and over. As much as I wanted to be inside her, my dick was going to have to wait. I wasn't done tasting her. Her fingernails dug into my back as I gently squeezed her breast and raked my teeth across her erect nipple. She squirmed and groaned as I lowered my mouth to her ribcage and down to her stomach. Each kiss, each tiny taste, made me hungry for more. A gasp hissed through her teeth as I lowered my head between her legs. I tenderly licked and kissed her inner thighs, then planted soft kisses on either side of her bikini bottoms. Her hips lifted off of the mattress as I pressed the palm of my hand firmly against her center, rhythmically rubbing her clit. I smiled when I saw that she was already wet. The anticipation of what I was going to do to her was getting to her just as much as it was getting to me.

"Oh, god. Don't stop," she pleaded.

"I have no intention of stopping, Josie." I kissed along her inner thigh. "I'm just getting started."

I reached for her bikini bottoms and slowly pulled them down her long, lean legs before tossing them to

135

the side. Seeing her lying there, bare and beautiful, took my breath away. She looked up at me, so trusting and full of desire, and I couldn't imagine wanting anything more. I slid my hands under her ass, pulling her closer as I lowered my mouth between her thighs. I started slow and steady, teasing her clit with my mouth. Her hips bucked against me, and I reveled in the effect I was having on her. Her little moans and whimpers filled the room, urging me on. I loved how her body responded to my every touch. I wanted to watch as her walls came crashing down, letting me see the Josie that was hidden behind them. I wanted to see her body twist and jolt as she came, to see her cheeks and chest flush red with desire. I wanted it all – even if it was for just one night.

After just a few more flicks of my tongue, her orgasm took hold, causing her entire body to quiver and shake uncontrollably. I continued to tease her relentlessly, intensifying her orgasm and fueling my own desire to be inside her. While she was still under the haze of her release, I pulled off my boxers and slipped on a condom, settling my body between her legs. We had both thought about that moment, dreamed about it, and it almost felt too good to be true. She looked up at me with her eyes full of desire as I brushed my throbbing cock along her entrance, driving us both wild with need.

"Mike… please," she pleaded as she wrapped her legs around me, pulling me forward. A deep growl vibrated through my chest as I drove deep inside her. At first my rhythm was slow and tender, giving her time to adjust to me, but when her nails dug into my back and her hips thrusted forward, I found myself craving more. I drove deeper… harder, but continued to keep a slow, gentle rhythm.

I could tell she was becoming frustrated when she tightened her legs around my waist and rocked against me, encouraging me to give her more. When I pulled back, she cried out, "Mike, please!"

"You're so fucking tight, Josie," I growled as I ground my hips against her. "Fuck!"

I thrust deeply, again and again, each move more intense than the last. Her eyes clenched shut and her head fell back as I continued to increase my rhythm. My piercing raked against her G spot, causing her to tense around me. I raked my teeth over her breast as I took her nipple in my mouth. Every nerve in her body seemed to explode with my touch. I was enjoying every single moment of watching her come undone, but my resistance was faltering. Her breath quickened as she clamped down around my cock, making it damn near impossible not to come. A deep groan vibrated through my throat as I continued to drive deep inside her. I could feel her imminent release and saw it on her face, so I thrusted harder, deeper, forcing her over the edge. Her hands dropped to her side and she fisted the sheets in her hands as her orgasm took hold. I fought to catch my breath, tried to fight it, but it was futile. My mind grew blank as my body took over. Her arms wrapped around my neck, and I felt her breath against my chest as I drove deeper inside her, finally giving into my own release.

Every muscle in my body started to relax as she began to softly kiss my neck and shoulder. I lowered myself onto the mattress and after I disposed of the condom, I pulled her over to my side. After pulling one of the covers over us, she settled in the crook of my arm and rested her head on my shoulder. Without looking in my direction, she whispered, "I don't know if I should say this, but I think I'm falling for you. If I haven't already fallen, like deep… way down into the well."

I wanted to tell her I felt the same about her, but knew I couldn't. "Falling for a guy like me is a bad idea, Josie."

"I don't know. Some pretty amazing things have come from a bad idea." She curled into my side and settled beneath the covers. "Like electricity. That whole kite-and-lightning thing was a totally bad idea, and look at us now. And then there's corn dogs and MoonPies."

"*MoonPies?*"

"Absolutely. Cookies and marshmallows aren't a good mix. You have to find just the right ratio of marshmallow to cookie. Too much of either, and it's just gross. They finally got it right, and then took it a step farther and dipped that sucker in chocolate. Now, that was a bad idea turned into a real piece of art."

"Mmm-hmm."

She got quiet for a moment as she trailed the lines

of my tattoo with the tip of her finger, and then she lifted her head and looked at me with a smile. "You never know. You could be *my* MoonPie."

Chapter 14

Josie

My body was still trying to recover from complete sensory overload as I lay there in his arms. I was in a state of pure bliss, and I couldn't imagine any place I'd rather be. I looked over at him, amazed at just how beautiful he was. There was no doubt I was attracted to the man. That was a given, but then any woman in her right mind would be attracted to all those rippling muscles and gorgeous face. And good lord, those eyes – his eyes were what dreams were made of. But it was more than just his looks I was drawn to. He was brilliant and charming in a way you wouldn't expect from a biker, and he was thoughtful and loving, even when he wasn't trying to be, like the day he took me to the farm. He knew I needed a break and took time out of his day to make me feel better. I loved that he was protective, not just with me but with everyone he cared about. Michael Davis had stolen my heart, but I couldn't tell him that, at least not yet. For now, I'd just consider him my sugary sweet.

He pulled me closer and gave me a tight squeeze as he chuckled. "I'm nobody's MoonPie, Josie."

"If you say so." Remembering an odd sensation I'd felt when we made love, I quickly lifted the blanket. My eyes slowly traveled below his waist, and then I spotted it: a silver stud stared right back at me, making me inhale quickly. Yep, he was pierced. My face burned with the heat of embarrassment as I mumbled, "Oh my god."

A low rumble of laughter vibrated through his chest. "You got something on your mind, sweetheart?"

"You have a piercing... on your.... I mean, I thought you were pierced down there, but I wasn't sure. Everything was moving kind of fast, you know, and uh, um... *Damn*."

"It's just a piercing. Nothing to get all worked up about."

When I finally realized I was still peering under the blanket like an idiot, I dropped the covers and fell back onto the bed. I was beyond embarrassed as I told him, "Yep, you're definitely a MoonPie."

"I've already told you, I'm nobody's MoonPie, baby. Trust me on that."

Thinking about cookies made my stomach growl. I looked over at the clock and couldn't believe it was already after six. "I'm starving."

"You wanna get a shower and then go grab a bite to eat?" Without answering, I eased up out of the bed and reached for my bathing suit. When I started to slip it back on, Big laughed. "I'll take that as a yes."

"What part of starving didn't you understand?" Once I had my suit back on, I leaned over the bed and kissed him lightly on the lips. "I'll be back in half an hour."

"I'll be ready."

I rushed out the door and up the elevator. For the first time in weeks, I felt good, really good, and I wanted to share it with Tristen. I wanted to tell her about everything, from the ride to the farm and all the things we'd done to get her back, but most of all, I wanted to tell her how very much I missed her. Just as I stepped into my room, I heard the faint sound of my cell phone ringing. I'd left it charging by the bed since I wasn't expecting any calls. When I looked down at the screen, I didn't recognize the number. I quickly answered, and my heart stopped when I heard the voice on the other end of the line.

"Josie?"

"Amanda?" My heart almost leapt out of my chest. "Is that you?"

"I only have a minute, Josie. I just wanted to tell you how sorry I am. I wish I could've done something…" Her voice was strained like she was on the brink of crying.

Remembering everything Big had told me about not tipping anyone off, I asked, "Done something about what? What's going on Amanda? Do you know where Tristen is?"

"You should know… she'll have everything she's ever wanted and more. These men are very wealthy." She took a deep breath. "They'll be good to her. Victor promised."

I felt my stomach twist into a knot when I realized

Amanda knew everything. She knew the Calaveras had my sister, and they were planning to auction her off. Damn. I had to know if she knew something we didn't, so I pushed, "I don't understand, Amanda. What men?"

"There are men who don't have time to date. They're good guys, but they're too busy with their careers, so… they…"

"So, they what, Amanda?"

"They pay a great deal of money to find the right girl. Tristen will make someone very happy, and she will have a life we only dream of."

Anger surged through me. There was no way Amanda was buying the load of bullshit she was throwing at me. "Is this something Tristen *wanted* to do, Amanda? Or was she forced into it?"

"She'll have nice clothes and fancy jewelry. And…"

"Just stop," I cut her off. "Do you have any idea what you've done, Amanda? You're talking about sex trafficking! There's no telling what these men will do to her! They'll force her to do all kinds of horrific things. God knows what! You got my sister involved in a nightmare, not some stupid dream!"

"No, Victor promised," she muttered.

"Victor is a damned liar."

"I'm so sorry, Josie, but I didn't have a choice," she muttered. "I… didn't want any of this to happen."

"Then, why? Why didn't you try to stop it?"

"Because of Lisa," she sobbed.

I felt absolutely no pity for this girl; only absolute anger. "What about Lisa? What did she do this time?"

"She's been seeing Victor for almost a year. She's in pretty deep with him. I think she actually loves the guy."

"And?"

"Well, he… he'd gotten a new shipment in, and she was trying to help him get it transported to their warehouse downtown. It would've been fine, but she got pulled over by the cops and her stash got confiscated."

"What does any of that have to do with Tristen?"

"She had to find a way to make that money back or they were going to kill her."

"And what about Victor?"

She cleared her throat and tried to remain calm. "He tried to fix it, but they blamed everything on Lisa. Said it was her fault for not being careful."

"You can't make my sister pay the consequences for *your* sister's mistake!"

"I don't have a choice. It's going to be fine… They will make sure she gets a good guy. He promised. I've gotta go. They can't know I contacted you. Just trust me… It will be okay."

"Amanda wait! Just tell me where she is!" I listened but got no response. "Amanda!"

Shit! I threw the phone down on the bed and screamed. I was louder than I'd intended, and two of Nitro's guys came crashing through my door. When they found me standing there completely unharmed, one of them asked, "Everything okay?"

"Everything's fine. I thought I saw a spider, but it was just a shadow." I motioned them towards the door. "You can go. I'm all good."

Once they were gone, I closed the door and headed into the bathroom. I stepped into the shower with my mind still focused on my conversation with Amanda. The tightness in my chest grew more intense as I went over and over everything she'd told me. It was like she almost believed the lies, liked she needed them to be true, but I could hear it in her voice: deep down, she knew the truth. She was exchanging Tristen's life for her sister's, plain and simple. By the time I got out of the shower, I was more determined than ever to find Tristen. I was ready for it all to be over. I was tired of being scared, tired of worrying if I would ever see my sister again, and I would do whatever it took to make it stop.

I dug through my bag and grabbed a pair of jeans and a black sweater. After I finished getting dressed and fixing my hair, I headed back down to Mike's room. I knocked on the door, and as soon as he opened it, I charged inside.

"I think we should go find Amanda." I reached for my phone and held it in front of him. "I've got her address in my contacts. We'll go over there, get her to tell us where they are keeping Tristen, and then we can—"

"Whoa. Slow down," he said as he walked over to me and placed his hands on my shoulders.

"This will work. I can get her to tell me—"

"No, Josie. We aren't going to Amanda. We aren't going anywhere. We're gonna stick to the plan, and by this time tomorrow, we will be on a plane headed home with your sister. You just need to be patient."

I groaned as I plopped down on the edge of the bed and said, "Okay."

"What brought all this on?" He looked down at me with concern.

"Amanda just called me." I saw the veins in his neck start to bulge, so I continued. "She just confirmed everything we already knew. I never let on that I knew what she was talking about, so she blabbed everything. She told me Victor took Tristen to settle some debt Lisa had with the cartel."

"Tristen never stood a chance."

"Nope. And Amanda tried to convince me that she was actually doing Tristen some kind of favor by doing this." I ran my fingers through my hair and sighed. "She said she'd have a life like we only dreamed of. Crazy, right?"

"I'm sure she was just trying to make you feel better."

"No, she was trying to make *herself* feel better. I didn't buy any of it and I let her know I wasn't falling for her lies." I huffed. "I'm sorry. I'm just so ready for all of this to be over."

He sat down beside me and slipped his arm around my waist. I leaned into him as he said, "It will be, soon. You'll see."

"I really hope so."

"You still up for dinner?" He smiled.

"How about something easy? Like a burger or something?" I suggested.

He stood up and reached for my hand. "Burger sounds good."

After we drove out to some little burger joint, he took me for a drive around, showing me some of the hot spots in town. I knew what he was doing. I didn't have to say the words for him to know how worried I was about Tristen and everything that could happen at that auction. He could sense it, and instead of trying to convince me that everything would be okay, he was trying to distract me from my thoughts.

It was working, until he got a text message.

I had no idea who'd sent it or what it said, but his mood quickly changed from easygoing and carefree to tense and intimidating. Without saying a word, he drove us back to the hotel and led me up to my room. Before he turned to leave, I looked up at him and smiled. "I had a really good time tonight… and *earlier*."

"Had a good time myself, but then, I always do when I'm with you." I felt my heart flutter at his words. He leaned towards me and lightly kissed me. "I've got some things to tend to, but if you need me, just let me know."

"I will."

"Get some rest. I'll check on you later tonight."

He started back towards the elevator and I waited until he stepped inside. I watched as the doors slowly started to close. Something was up. It was written all over his face when he read that text message. I wondered if something had happened with Tristen, if there was some hitch he decided to keep from me, and I considered trying to find out for myself what was going on. I thought about trying to hack into his phone to find the message or possibly following him when he left my room, but something told me to leave it. Something in my gut told me I could trust Mike. Whatever was going on, I knew in my heart that he'd take care of it. I liked that feeling of security I felt whenever I thought about him. Thinking back on my mother and that cliff, I couldn't help but wonder how something that felt so good could be so wrong. I was beginning to think I just didn't care. I had to stop lying to myself. Pretending he wasn't getting to me was becoming harder by the minute. He's just too damn irresistible. I want him, and I can't keep pretending that I don't.

Chapter 15

Big

I couldn't remember when I'd had such a good night – or afternoon, for that matter – and I wasn't ready for it to end. I'd never met anyone like Josie. I knew from the start she was going to change my life. I just didn't know what kind of change she had in mind. Without her even knowing it, she held that ability in the palm of her hand, and it was up to her how she used it. For the time being, I would have to wait and see. Stitch sent me a message that there was news, so I had to cut the night short. I left her room and headed down to the bar to find him. As soon as I walked into the room and spotted him sitting in the corner, I knew something was wrong – really fucking wrong. His elbows were propped on the table and his head rested in the palms of his hands. When I sat down beside him, he ran his fingers down his face and groaned. It was one of those deep, pissed off kind of groans, sounding more like a mad dog growling. "You gonna tell me what the hell is going on or am I supposed to guess?"

Before he could answer, Nitro walked up and sat down next to me. He looked over at Stitch with a concerned look. "Have you told him?"

"One of you better get to talking," I warned.

"There might be a problem," Nitro started. "I got a

call about an hour ago from a Gordo. He said there'd been a change of plan, and they are moving the time of the auction to later tonight. Told me to wait for their call."

"Did he say why?"

"Not exactly. I asked if there was a problem, and they said they had everything under control. That this kind of thing happens from time to time. Of course, I wouldn't know. This shit is all new to me."

"What about your contact?"

"Haven't been able to reach him." That wasn't a good sign, and I could tell from Nitro's blank expression that he was just as concerned about it as I was.

Stitch leaned forward. "I don't like it. Not one fucking bit."

"I don't either. This is a red flag, brother. Something's up with this shit." I leaned back in my chair and turned to Stitch. "What's your take on this?"

"I think shit is about to hit the fan. Something is up with these guys. I don't know for certain, but I'd say a lot of planning goes into these things. They've got men from all over coming in to buy these women. A lot of money is at stake. They wouldn't go changing shit around unless someone was putting heat on them."

After taking a sip of his bourbon, Stitch continued. "Or this whole thing could be a fucking setup. Someone could've tipped them off that we're here, and they're trying to kill us off."

Big

"Maybe, but I doubt it," Nitro started. "They knew where we are. If they wanted us, they could get to us anytime. Why go to all this trouble?"

"Who knows, but I figure they'd do just about anything to make sure we don't fuck with their auction," Stitch snapped. "Whether you like it or not, these fuckers are shady as shit, brother. You can't trust any of them."

"Maybe not, but we've got no choice. If we don't see this thing through, we're leaving here without Tristen."

"That's not an option." I'd given my word to Cotton, and after all the hell Josie had been through over the past few weeks, there was no way in hell we were leaving LA without her sister.

"Then we make this thing work." Nitro motioned to the waitress for a drink. "We stick to the plan. You'll go in with me. Stitch and my boys will wait in the SUV. Any sign of trouble, and they'll know what to do."

"How the fuck are we supposed to know there's trouble, Nitro? When they bring your big asses out in body bags?"

"I've got that covered," I assured him. "Any idea where this shit is going down?"

Nitro shook his head. "Said they'd give me all the details when they called back."

"Then we'll just have to wait for the call." When I stood up, Stitch followed suit. "Let us know as soon as you hear from them. I'm going to do a little research and see if I can find out if there are any investigations going on in the area."

"With these guys around, I bet there's always some kind of investigation going on, but let me know if you find anything." When we started to leave, Nitro called, "Your turn to put on a show, brother. Gonna need to wear that suit tonight."

"What suit?"

His lips curled into a smirk. "The Armani I sent up to your room. Wear it."

"Seriously? A fucking suit."

He leaned back in his chair and crossed his arms. "Just a small sacrifice."

I turned and started to leave. "Fuck off, Nitro."

"And the tie!"

I went back to my room, and just like Nitro had warned, there was a garment bag hanging on my closet door. I unzipped it and found a black suit with a white dress shirt and a royal blue tie. Damn. I hated fucking monkey suits. Choosing to ignore it for the moment, I pulled out my laptop and started digging. If the cops were on to the auction, it wouldn't be good, but it would be a hell of a lot better than the Calaveras being on to us. After forty-five minutes of searching, I found what I was looking for. I was about to message Stitch with what I'd found when there was a knock at my door. I opened it and found Josie standing on the other side. She was wearing a baggy pair of gray sleep pants that fell low on her hips and a fitted black tank top. Her hair was down around her shoulders, and she wasn't wearing any makeup. She was absolutely stunning.

"Is everything okay?" Her breath was shallow and her shoulders were rigid and full of tension. "I know you're busy, but I was worried something might be wrong."

"Never too busy for you." I reached for her hand, leading her into my room. I hated to lie to her, but there was no sense in freaking her out any more than she already was. "Sorry about earlier. Didn't mean to make you worry."

"Don't be sorry. I know you have a lot to do to get things ready for tomorrow night." When she mentioned tomorrow night, I felt a twinge of guilt for not telling her about the change in plan, but I knew it was best to leave it.

"You need to get some rest, Josie."

"I can't sleep." She looked up at me with her eyes filled with sadness, making my heart feel like it was ripped from my chest. "I can't stop thinking about her. I keep trying to tell myself that she's okay, and half the time I actually believe it. Then, I think about all those awful articles I read, except now they aren't faceless names. Now, every one of them is Tristen. I keep imagining all the horrible things they might be doing to her."

Tears trickled down her face, and I would do anything to take her hurt away. "Baby, you can't keep doing that to yourself. I know you're worried, but this will all be over soon."

She stepped over to me and tilted her head back as her eyes locked on mine. "I need to forget. Just for a little while. The only time I don't drive myself crazy is when I'm with you. Please, Mike. Help me forget."

Seeing that look in her eyes and being so damn close to her, there was no way I could tell her no, so I dropped my mouth to hers and kissed her long and hard. Her mouth was warm and wet, and all her little moans and whimpers made me ache with need. When she pulled her tank over her head, exposing her perfect, round breasts, I was done. I had to have her. I leaned over her and watched the goosebumps rise along her skin as I began to trace the slope of her breast with my fingertips. She was perfect – every damned inch of her – and I couldn't help but imagine a lifetime with her in my arms, making love over and over again. I trailed kisses down the curve of her neck as my hands roamed over her body. Her scent was intoxicating, and I was overcome with need. I slipped her pajama bottoms and panties down past her ankles, then lowered her onto the bed.

I looked down at her, amazed once again at her beauty, and realized there was nothing I wouldn't do for this woman. Without even knowing it, she'd stolen something from me, something I thought I'd never give up again without a fight: my heart. But I found myself wanting her to have it, knowing I'd never feel this way about any other woman.

I quickly removed my clothes, slid on a condom, and eased myself between her legs. I watched with wonder as her back arched off the bed when my cock brushed against her heat. *Damn*. I loved how her body responded instantly to my touch. I couldn't get enough. I lowered my mouth to her breast, nipping and sucking as I slid inside her, quickly finding the spot that drove her wild. With the sounds of her moans echoing through the room, I placed my hands on her hips and held her in place while I continued to drive deep inside. Watching her body twist and jolt beneath me made my cock throb with an uncontrollable need.

I placed my mouth close to her ear and whispered, "I'll never get enough of you, Josie Carmichael. Never."

Without saying a word, she pressed her lips to mine in a possessive, demanding kiss and wrapped her legs around my waist, forcing me deeper inside her. There was no doubt she wanted me just as much as I wanted her, and I had every intention of giving her all I had to give. I spent the next hour making love to her, burning every inch of her body into my memory. Knowing there was no way to know what the future held for us, I wanted to remember every moment, every touch, so I'd always have some part of her with me, no matter what happened in the hours to come.

As soon as I laid down next to her, she curled into my side, and the room suddenly became oddly quiet. I looked down at her and smiled when I noticed she'd fallen asleep. I couldn't help but stare at her, feeling in complete awe of just how beautiful she looked lying there, so peaceful and angelic. Her dreams had taken over, making all her worries seem to disappear. I could've stayed there all night just staring at her, but fate had other plans. My phone started ringing, and I quickly grabbed it from the bedside table before it woke her. As soon as I answered, Nitro said, "Time to saddle up and move out."

"I'll be up in ten."

I hung up the phone and groaned as I eased myself out of the bed. I took the garment bag and headed into the bathroom to get dressed. After twenty minutes of trying to get my fucking tie on, I went back to the room and grabbed my duffle bag. Josie was still sleeping soundly. There wasn't a point in waking her. We were running short on time, and since we hadn't been able to hack into the security feed, there was nothing she could do to help us. Figuring the sleep would do her good, I wrote her a note to let her know where we'd gone and that I'd be calling in a few hours. I kissed her gently on her temple and headed upstairs to meet Nitro and Stitch. When I walked in, they were all set on go. From the look on his face, Stitch obviously found the suit as ridiculous as I did. "Don't say a fucking word."

"Wasn't gonna," he snickered. "Nothing I could say could insult you any more than that suit does."

Ignoring him, I reached in my duffle bag. "How long do we have?"

"The bar is about twenty minutes from here," Nitro

answered.

"Bar?" I asked as I grabbed the miniaturized in-ear receivers and handed one to him.

"Gordo said they have a basement." Nitro took the earpiece and slipped it into his ear while I tucked the microphone in the inner corner of his lapel.

Once I was done, I put mine on, then handed Stitch his earpiece. "With these, you'll be able to hear everything that goes on while we're inside."

"Got it." After he placed it in his ear, Stitch turned to me. "Let's get this thing done."

Nitro's men were waiting for us downstairs and followed us out to the SUV. It was almost two a.m. when we pulled up to the address Gordo had given Nitro. When I caught the name of the bar, I grumbled, "You've gotta be kidding me."

Nitro shook his head. "Now, I've seen it all. Who'd ever think they'd have this damned thing at a fucking sushi place."

"Nothing these guys do surprises me anymore." I turned off the engine and turned to Nitro. "You ready?"

"Born ready, brother."

I got out of the truck, and once I'd grabbed the briefcase of cash, I followed him up to the door where we were greeted by two Hispanic men with matching ink and menacing stares. Without confirming our identity, one of them opened the door and motioned us inside. As soon as we stepped inside, two more guards were there waiting for us. After a thorough pat-down, one of them turned to the bar and called, "Yo, esé. They're good."

A heavyset man with a wide, creepy grin waved us over. When we got to the bar, he smiled and said, "Can I get you two a drink? I've got a bottle of tequila with your name on it."

I figured Nitro recognized the man's voice from their previous phone calls when he said, "Thanks, Gordo. I'll take a shot."

Gordo took the bottle and filled two shot glasses full to the brim. "If you're ready, we'll head downstairs to meet the others."

Nitro downed the shot and took the other in his hand. "All set."

We followed him over to a side door and down a flight of stairs. Once we got to the bottom, he motioned us forward and we continued down a hallway where the light was just a soft glow. It was too dark to get a good look at anyone who was coming or going; everyone was, just moving silhouettes as they passed by. I glanced behind me, thinking if anything went wrong, we were screwed. There was no way in hell Stitch and Nitro's boys could get to us in time, but we had no choice but to move forward. Bad seventies music was blaring from the end of the hall, and as soon as we stepped inside, my stomach turned. The room was dark, except for the light that was shining on the girls. They were lined up against the back wall with their hands bound behind their backs. My blood ran cold when I spotted Tristen standing at the end of the line. They had her dressed in a cheap, bright red string bikini, and like the others, her hair and makeup was overdone, making them all look like typical prostitutes. Their eyes were glassed over, making them look like something out of a horror flick as several men circled around them. They looked like fucking sharks as they checked out the merchandise, and I had to fight the urge to kill each and every one of them. Nitro signaled me to wait, while he joined the others, doing what he could to blend in.

Once I got to the back corner, I got a better look and at just the sight of them standing there, my chest tightened, making the air feel thick as I tried to breath. Their ages ranged from around twelve to twenty, with every flavor you could imagine, from Nordic blondes with blues eyes, to voluptuous dark-skinned Hispanic girls and even a few almond-eyed Asians. They seemed completely out of it as the men hovered over them, grabbing their breasts and asses as they examined every inch of their bodies. Hell, they were even checking their goddamned teeth. Some might say it was just the nature of the beast – men fulfilling their most carnal desires – but I found it barbaric. I felt ashamed to be in the same room with these motherfuckers. I glanced over at Nitro and couldn't imagine how he had the strength to talk to these men like they were long lost pals. Through my earpiece, I listened as he played the game, talking and laughing, carrying on like he was a hungry predator just like the rest of them. My heart started to race when a couple of the men stopped as they got to Tristen. It was clear she'd caught their attention. They spent several minutes eyeballing her and whispering back and forth. After several minutes, they finally moved on to the next girl, but not before they put their fucking hands all over her. Over the headset, I heard Nitro whisper, "Breathe, brother."

When Nitro finally made his way over to her, and while she was in a daze, she looked at him, really looked at him. He didn't say anything, but an odd expression crossed his face as he stood there in front of her. They both looked like they'd been caught up in some kind of spell as they stared at each other, but it was quickly broken when another man approached them. Trying to seem uninterested in her, Nitro moved on to the next few girls. He continued through all the rest, making sure to pay close attention to each, and then he joined the others as they waited for the bidding to begin. Looking at them all standing there, it was hard to believe these guys were actually buying these women. While a few of them looked like your typical mafia guys with their fancy suits, expensive watches, and bad comb-overs, there was nothing typical about the others. The thin guy with the horn-rimmed glasses and a stiff brown suit reminded me of my seventh grade science teacher, only this guy had an eerie gleam in his eye, one that made my skin crawl just by looking at him. They all gave me a bad vibe, but there was one other guy that got under my skin. He was heavyset, reminding me of Jabba the Hutt with his bald head and large, rolling belly. His sinister laugh echoed around the room as he said vile things about each of the girls, and I wanted nothing more than to put a fucking bullet between his eyes.

A hush fell across the room as one of the Hispanic men walked in front of the girls and glared out into the crowd. An evil smile curled across his face as he said, "Let's not keep these lovely ladies waiting. I'm sure they are all eager to find out which one of you will be taking them home."

The first few girls went quickly. He walked over to each one, taking the bids and becoming more arrogant with each large sum that was offered. When he came up to the young girl, her blue eyes filled with tears as she listened to him talk about her virginity and pureness. Even through all the makeup they threw on her, anyone could see that she was just a child, barely even developed. Bile rose to my throat as I listened to him carry on, and I could only imagine the horror she must've been feeling.

He ran his hand down her back. "A real beauty, amigos. Ready to please. Just look at her... I can smell her fresh pussy from here."

Jabba the Hut cleared his throat and made an offer. "I'll do seventy-five."

As soon as the words came out of his mouth, the Hispanic man's face turned red. "*Cabrón miserable. Debería patearte el culo*. Going to have to do better than that, amigo."

A bidding war ensued between Jabba and the teacher, each of them trying to outdo the other, but eventually the price got too high at two hundred grand, and the brown suit bailed out. I thought it was over, thinking that fat bastard was going to get her. My heart ached for the young girl when I thought of the terrible things the man would do to her, hearing him boast about making her his, but we were all caught by surprise when Nitro cleared his throat and shouted, "I'll give you three hundred."

I had no idea how much money Nitro had brought in the briefcase. I wasn't there when he withdrew the money from his account, so I was worried he wouldn't have enough to cover Tristen, too. Over the mic, I warned, "*Nitro.*"

The speaker smiled. "Three hundred is a fair price for a virgin *puta.*" He looked over at the heavyset man. "Care to go higher?"

"Three fifty."

Ignoring my warning, Nitro replied, "Four hundred."

"Fuck. No pussy is worth that bullshit." The fat man stepped back and growled, "Take the bitch."

Two other girls were auctioned off before they got to Tristen. I knew from the panic on her face that the drugs were starting to wear off. She held her head high as the man approached her, grabbing the back of her long, blonde hair as he said, "*Puta rubia con ojos azules.* Blonde and blue, my friends. A real catch. Let's start the bidding at fifty."

The price quickly rose to one hundred and fifty without Nitro even making an offer. He waited until the bids started to slow before he stepped forward. "Two hundred."

"My friend knows what he wants," he snickered. "Two hundred on the table." Relief washed over me when the room fell silent, but it was short lived.

Suddenly, the man with the brown suit spoke up, "I'll do two fifty."

The Hispanic man's lips curled into a nasty grin as he stepped over to Tristen and ran his hand down her back, squeezing tightly when he reached her ass. "She's a real beauty, my friends. Surely she would make any one of you feel great pleasure tonight."

As soon as he finished talking, another bid came in. "Three hundred."

My chest tightened as I waited for Nitro to counter, but nothing came out of his mouth. He just sat there completely silent as the other men heckled back and forth. Losing patience, I growled into the mic, "*Nitro.*"

Ignoring me, he continued to remain silent and seemed completely unfazed as another bid was made. "Three fifty."

"Now, we're talking," the Hispanic man boasted.

I was about to have a complete come-apart when Nitro finally cleared his throat and announced, "Five hundred."

A hush fell over the room as the men turned to face

Nitro. He made no acknowledgment to their hateful glares as he waited to see if another bid came in. When nothing else was said, the Hispanic man nodded. "Five hundred it is."

Once all the girls were sold, Nitro signaled to me to bring the briefcase over to him. The money was quickly counted, and the girls were brought over to Nitro. "Thank you for your business, Mr. Nitro."

"Same to you."

Gordo grabbed Tristen by the arm and tugged her over to Nitro while another man brought the young girl over to the back corner to me. "Take them out the back entrance."

Nitro nodded and started walking towards the door. He'd only taken a step, when Tristen started to resist, fighting with all her might to break free from his hold. He pressed the tips of his fingers firmly against her forearm, forcing her to stop. Through the mic I heard him say, "You want to stay here with them?" He paused as he waited for her response. "I didn't think so. I know you're scared, Tristen, but you're going to have to trust me." At the sound of her name, I saw her eyes widen with surprise. "If I can't save you, I can't save me. It's up to you how this thing goes down."

She gave him a slight nod and took a staggered step towards him. When she finally noticed me standing there, her eyes widened with surprise. The realization of what was really happening dawned on her and I could see the relief in her eyes as she stared at me. I brought my finger up to my lips, letting her know to stay quiet, but it was all too much. Her step started to waiver. She was too exhausted, too drugged to continue walking on her own, so Nitro scooped her up into his arms, cradling her against his chest as he continued walking through the door. He lowered his mouth to her ear and whispered to her, but the words were too muffled for me to hear.

Once she had settled down, Nitro started walking out of the room. He hadn't made it far when the Jabba the Hut asshole started shouting. "You arrogant piece of shit. You think you can just come in here, take what's mine, and get away with it?"

With Tristen still in his arms, Nitro glared at him. "I bought her. She's mine."

"Do you know who I am?"

"Don't know, and don't really give a fuck. Step the fuck off," Nitro growled.

"You fucked with the wrong man, asshole. I'll end you!" When he took an angry step forward, I eased the kid behind me and stepped in front of Nitro, blocking the douchbag's path. "Move!"

"Not happening, mister. You need to leave it. The deal is done."

"I'm not leaving a damn thing. That little cunt was handpicked for me, and that asshole swindled me." He took another step forward, trying to bypass me when he spotted the kid. "Come here, you little bitch. You're mine!"

When he reached out for her, I lost all my restraint and reared back my fist, punching that dickhead with all my might square in the throat, then again in his enormous gut. He toppled over as the sounds of his choking filled the room. I bent down towards his head and growled, "Told you to back the fuck off, you perverted motherfucker. You even think about touching that little girl again, and I will break every fucking bone in your hand."

Still gasping for breath, he brought his hands up to his throat, tugging frantically at his collar as he tried to take a breath. His bodyguard finally noticed the commotion and charged in my direction. Adrenaline rushed through my veins as I watched him approach. I quickly surveyed the room, making sure none of the others were going to jump in as I waited for him to get closer. I heard Stitch's voice calling over the headset, "Mike… just say the word and we'll be there."

Without answering, I slammed my fist into the bodyguard's jaw, then threw another three hard punches to his gut. Thankfully, he wasn't in much better shape than his employer, so he dropped like a ton of fucking bricks.

When he didn't get up, I looked back over at Nitro. "Let's get the fuck out of here."

I reached for the kid's hand and followed Nitro and Tristen up the stairs. Before we got outside, I took off my suit jacket and wrapped it around her as I said, "It's going to be all right, kid. We aren't going to hurt you."

Big

"You promise?

"I promise. We just want to get you out of here and away from these men. You good with that?"

"Mmm-hmm."

"What's your name kid?"

"Lauren."

"Ok, Lauren. We'll get you back to your folks as soon as we can."

"No! Please," she cried. "Please don't make me go back there."

Surprised by her reaction, I told her, "We'll get you somewhere safe, then. I give you my word on that."

When we got back to the SUV, Nitro opened the back door and said, "Move."

His guy got out of the truck and waited as Nitro settled inside with Tristen still in his arms. I handed the girl to Stitch and got in the driver's seat. Once we were rolling, I turned back to Nitro and asked, "You got any idea what we're going to do with the kid?"

"No fucking idea, but there was no way in hell I was going to let that fat bastard have her. Work it out with Cotton. Either find her folks or keep her. I don't give a fuck."

"You just paid four hundred grand for that kid."

"I did. And I'd do it again. I couldn't live with myself thinking about the life she'd have with him. Enough said. Now drive. We need to get the hell out of here."

I looked back and I almost couldn't believe that

Tristen was sitting in Nitro's lap. We'd actually managed to get her back, and she was okay. She laid her head on his shoulder and closed her eyes as she whispered, "Thank you. Thank you. Thank you."

Chapter 16
Josie

With one phone call, I felt the weight of the world lifted from my shoulders. They'd gotten Tristen and were on their way back to the hotel to get me. I jumped out of bed and was surprised to see that Big had already packed up and cleared the room. Knowing we'd be rushed for time, I hurried upstairs and, after I changed my clothes, I threw everything into my duffle bag and headed downstairs. My mind was bombarded with questions as I got on the elevator. It was the first time I'd had a minute to think since Big called. He hadn't told me much, only that they had her and we all needed to leave town immediately. I wanted to believe that it was all over, but deep down I knew it was just beginning. My heart ached for my sister. Even if she'd gotten lucky and they hadn't beaten and raped her, it would still take her time to get over being kidnapped and drugged. Only time would tell just how bad things would get, and I just prayed that she'd have the strength to see it through.

When I spotted the black SUV pulling up to the curb, I rushed outside and met Big as he was opening his door. "Where is she? Is she okay?"

"She's still a little out of it, but she's okay. She's sleeping in the back."

Big slowly opened the back door, and I couldn't fight back the tears as I looked at my sister. Her head was leaning back on Nitro's shoulder as he held her protectively in his arms. Trying his best not to disturb her, he slowly eased out of the truck, then carefully settled her back in the seat alone. Big was right; she was out of it, but my sister was sitting right there in front of me. I could see her. She was just a few feet away, but my mind just couldn't believe it. I was afraid she was just some figment of my imagination, so I gently placed the palm of my hand on her cheek. As soon as I touched her, felt the warmth of her skin against my hand, I knew she was real. Relief flooded over me as I stood there crying, watching my sister sleep. For the first time in weeks, I didn't have to worry whether my sister was alive or dead. I didn't have to wonder if I'd ever get her back, and I owed it all to Big and Nitro.

Feeling overcome with gratitude, I got out of the truck. I was about to go thank them all when a second SUV pulled in behind us. I turned to get a better look and saw that Nitro's men were sitting inside. Thinking he must've decided to drive back on his own, I didn't pay much attention to it and walked over to Big. Just as I got over to them, I heard Nitro say, "Tell him to keep his fucking money. I'm keeping her."

"Nitro," Big growled.

"I don't want to fucking hear it, Big. I'm the one who walked in there, put my fucking money on the table, and I'm leaving here with her whether he gives the okay or not. He didn't take care of her... not the way he should have. If he had, none of this shit would've happened."

"That's bullshit and you know it."

Nitro's voice softened. "This is what I know. The girl passed out in that truck. The girl who's been through hell and back... she's gonna need help. *Real* fucking help to get through this thing without being totally fucked up. I'm gonna do whatever it takes to get her that help."

I could see the true concern in Nitro's face, but there was no way in hell I was going to let him take Tristen, not when I just got her back. I stepped between them and said, "She's not going anywhere with you. She's coming back home with me."

Big added, "We can get her the help she needs."

Determination filled his eyes. "Maybe so, but I'm not taking any chances. She deserves fucking better than what she's gotten in the past. A lot fucking better, and I'm gonna make sure she gets it."

Whether he'd meant to or not, his words hit me hard. I'd never gotten over the guilt of leaving her after my parents' death, and it was hard not to agree with Nitro; she did deserve better.

Seeing that he wasn't wavering, I asked, "And just where do you plan on taking her?"

"Got a place I know that will see to it that she gets off the drugs and will help her deal with the addiction."

I shook my head with confusion. "What makes you

think she's got an addiction? She's never had an issue with drugs."

"She will now. They've been pumping her full of shit since the day they took her. Now, her body thinks it needs it. Before she fell asleep, her fingers were already starting to twitch, so the withdrawals are coming."

I was trying to be strong, but my voice cracked as I pleaded, "But I just got her back."

"Not trying to be a dick here, Josie, but this isn't about you. This is about your sister, and getting her the help she's gonna need. Whether any of you like it or not, I'm gonna see that she gets it."

"I'm not leaving my sister!"

"Then get your ass in that truck 'cause she's going with me." Nitro motioned to his men and they immediately got out. Moments later, they had Tristen settled in the back of their SUV.

Stunned, I looked over at Big, hoping for some kind of argument and thinking he'd tell Nitro that he couldn't run off with my sister, but I got nothing from him – just a soul-searching stare. "Aren't you going to say something about all this?"

"Nothing to say, Josie. He's right."

I sighed with aggravation. "How the hell can he be right? He's going to take her away from me!"

He took a step towards me and placed his hands on my shoulders. "He's not taking her from you, Josie. You gotta think about this. He's trying to help her. Without him, she wouldn't even be here. I trust him, Josie, and you should too."

"I can't leave her. Not now."

"No one is asking you to."

His words knocked the breath from my lungs. It wasn't what he said that hurt, but what he didn't say. There were no reassuring words letting me know he didn't like the idea of me leaving and no promises that he'd be in touch; only silence. I paused, staring into his eyes, searching for some unsaid plea for me to stay, but his gaze flickered to the ground. Trying my best to fight the feeling of rejection that crept up inside me, I lifted up on my tiptoes and gently kissed him on the lips. "Thank you… for everything."

Heartbroken, I turned and started back towards Nitro's truck. As much as I wanted him to, he didn't call out to me. He didn't try to stop me. He remained silent as I opened the truck door and got inside. I fought the urge to glance back at him, knowing it would hurt too much. I'd never know if he was looking at me with pain in his eyes. I'd never know if he was struggling with the fact that I was leaving or if he ever really cared at all. Either way, my heart couldn't take it, so I turned and focused on my sister. She was the only thing that mattered now. It was up to me to see to it that Nitro kept his word and got her the help she needed. Everything else would have to wait – including the burning ache I felt in my heart.

I hadn't been sitting there long when Nitro opened the truck, and as soon as he tossed my bag into the back seat, he sat behind the wheel. Even though I knew he had good intentions, it was hard not to be angry with him. "Where is this place you are taking her?"

"Out in Arizona. They're the best."

"Nitro?" He turned to face me with a blank expression. "Why are you doing this?"

From the way his eyes shifted to the backseat, I could see that it was a question he wasn't ready to answer, and honestly, I didn't think he knew why he was doing all this for a girl he didn't even know. "Just know in my gut it's the right thing to do."

There was something in his voice, a sincerity I didn't expect from him, and it was then that I finally got it. "You care about her, don't you?"

The man who always seemed unfazed by the world around him started the truck and turned his attention to the road in front of him. "I guess I do."

A half an hour later, we were at the airport sitting in some private jet. It was just a small plane with seven captains' chairs, but it was still a private jet. I was glad we didn't have to deal with any crowds, especially when Tristen started to come around. I'd given her some of my clothes to put on, hoping it might help her relax, but she was too far gone to understand what was going on. Her eyes widened with panic as she looked around. "Where are we?"

"You're on an airplane, sweetie. Everything's fine. We're getting you out of here."

"Josie." Her voice was weak. She looked so frail

and unlike the sister I'd always known. The spark in her eyes was gone, and she was so pale that her skin almost seemed transparent. "What's going on?"

"We're taking you out of here and away from those bad men who took you."

"What about Lauren?" she shrieked. "What happened to Lauren?"

I'd never heard her mention anyone by that name, so I had no idea who she was talking about. "Who's Lauren?"

"The little girl… long black hair and blue eyes. She was there with me." She was on the brink of becoming hysterical. "I promised I wouldn't leave without her."

"I don't know—" I started.

"We got her," Nitro interrupted. "She's fine."

"Oh, thank goodness." She settled back in her chair as she looked at Nitro. She studied him for a moment, and then whispered, "I remember you…. You were there."

"I was." He placed his hand on her knee. "Cotton sent me. I was there to bring you home."

"I thought I'd never get out of there. I was so scared."

I unbuckled my seatbelt and went over to her, wrapping my arms around her as she wept. "I'm so sorry sweetie. I know it must have been horrible."

"They had me in this room for days, Josie… and I couldn't understand anything they were saying to me. I tried to get away, but they… they kept me chained to the wall. And the drugs…" She sobbed. "They kept shooting that stuff into my veins. I begged them to stop… promised to be good, but they wouldn't stop."

"I'm right here." I felt so helpless. I wanted to take all her pain away, but all I could do was hold her and try to comfort her the only way I knew how. "It's over, sweetie. You don't have to worry about those people anymore."

"It's not over, Josie. It'll never be over… not for me." She shook her head and sobbed. "They're everywhere, Josie. I see their faces every time I close my eyes. I feel them touching me… hear them shouting at me… even though they are miles away."

"It won't be like that forever." I leaned back and looked her in the eye. "You just need some time. You'll see. It will get better."

Tristen looked down at the blanket she was wrapped in and groaned, "I really need a shower."

Nitro smiled. "It won't be much longer."

"Can we make one stop before we get there?" A curious look crossed Tristen's face as she waited for his answer.

"What kind of stop?"

"I just need to run into a convenience store. It won't take me long. Just need to grab something."

Nitro didn't try to hide the fact that he was suspicious. Like me, he was probably wondering if she was going to try to get one last fix before going into rehab. "You're gonna need to give me more than that."

Big

Her eyes dropped to her hands as she wrung them nervously in her lap. "It's my hair."

"What about your hair?"

"It's one of the reasons they took me… They kept saying, '*Ella tiene cabello rubio y ojos azules.*' They said I was going to make them a lot of money."

"She has blonde hair and blue eyes?"

"I don't want to have blonde hair anymore. I hate it. I need it to be gone," she muttered.

He nodded with understanding. "We can take care of that, but we'll do it right. I'll have someone come to your room and do it for you."

Nitro continued to amaze me with his unexpected kindness and understanding. I never expected that a man like him would have an actual soft side, but something about my sister brought it out in him. I liked that she had that kind of effect on him and hoped it would continue until she was better. When the plane landed, there was a car waiting for us, and after a thirty-minute drive, we pulled into the San Vista Rehabilitation Facility. With its large water fountains and beautiful tall columns, it looked more like a vacation resort than a drug treatment center. As soon as we parked the car, two nurses came out and helped us get Tristen to her room.

"I'll head downstairs while you get her settled." Nitro placed a bag on the edge of the bed. "Get her a shower and changed. Everything you'll need is in the bag."

When he turned to leave, Tristen went to him and wrapped her arms around his neck, hugging him tightly. She slowly released him and looked up at him with tears in her eyes. "I don't know how I'll ever be able to thank you for all of this."

With a quick wink and a coy, little smile, he replied, "You just did."

With that, he turned and walked out of the door. Tristen stood there staring aimlessly at the door before she started towards the bathroom. "You know... I don't think there'll be a shower long enough to get the feeling of filth off me."

I followed her into the bathroom and turned on the hot water. Steam quickly filled the room. I looked at Tristen and found her staring into the mirror. "For tonight, let's just focus on the makeup and bad hair. The other is going to take some time."

"I don't even recognize myself anymore." Her fingers trembled as she started to remove her clothes. "I know nothing's really changed. I'm still me, but I feel so... different."

I knew she was hurting, but I truly believed it when I told her, "You *are different.* You've been through hell and back, and you survived it all. You're *stronger* now, *wiser,* and hopefully you'll be able to look back on this day and know you beat them."

"Somehow, this doesn't feel like winning," she scoffed as she stepped into the shower.

"Maybe not now, but someday. You'll see."

B Chapter 17 **Big**

When Stitch and I left the hotel, we decided to bypass the airport altogether. We didn't have a ticket for Lauren and weren't prepared for the questions they might ask, so we headed back to Washington in the rental. The last few hours were a blur. Even after all the mile markers we'd passed, my mind was still focused on the hurt look on Josie's face when she kissed me goodbye. I knew letting her go was the right thing to do, but it still cut to the core. She'd gotten to me in a way no one ever had, and seeing her take off in Nitro's truck just about broke me. I wanted to stop her and claim her right there in that fucking parking lot, but it wasn't the right time or place. Whether I liked it or not, I had to be patient.

I'd tried to focus on the road ahead, but she was still on my mind when Stitch asked, "You reckon Cotton calmed down by now?"

"Doubt it, but not much we can do about that now." I'd called Cotton when we first left LA to let him know what had gone down with Nitro. The conversation didn't go as well as I'd hoped.

"We decided to drive back... We got ourselves a tag-along."

"Gonna need more than that, Big."

"It's one of the girls at the auction. She's just a kid… Nitro, kind of bought her."

"Bought her? What the fuck are you talking about?" he growled. *Bringing a kid back wasn't part of the plan. Nothing that had happened in those past few hours had been planned, but it's how it all played out. Getting Cotton to accept that wasn't easy. Eventually, after a great deal of explaining, I managed to make Cotton understand why leaving the kid behind wasn't an option. Trying to explain why Nitro had taken Tristen wasn't so easy.*

"What the fuck do you mean he took her?"

"He took Tristen and Josie with him."

"Where the hell did he take them?"

"He didn't exactly say."

"Goddammit, Mike. Tell me what the fuck he did *say!"* he snapped.

"They'd been pumping drugs into Tristen since the day they took her. She was all fucked up, Prez. A fucking nightmare. He saw that she was gonna need help and said he was going to make sure she got it. He didn't give an exact location."

"What made that motherfucker think he could just take off with her without going through me first?" His voice was filled with anger as he shouted into the phone.

"Nitro has a mind of his own, Prez," I tried to explain. *"And in his head, he thought he was doing the*

right thing for her."

"Don't give a fuck what he thought. He knows damn well he comes to me before he makes any decisions like this, especially when it involves someone from the club." He growled with frustration. "I'll deal with Nitro. Get your ass back and be thinking about what the hell you're gonna do with that kid."

He was pissed, and I couldn't blame him. He was our president, and he took his role seriously. Nitro had double-crossed him *and* the club by taking Tristen. It was going to take some time for Cotton and the others to understand why he'd done it. As for me, I think she got to him. Not sure how, but something happened between them at that auction, some kind of silent connection, and while I didn't understand it, it meant something to him.

When I pulled through the gate, I turned to Stitch. "Gonna have to figure out what to do with Lauren." I opened the door and stepped out of the truck. When I opened the back door to get her, I told him, "We're gonna have to find out where she came from and see if there's somebody who can take her in."

"I don't know, man. You said she seemed pretty freaked when you mentioned getting her back to her folks. Probably a reason she doesn't want to go back there." He got out and headed to the trunk to grab our bags.

"Either way, we gotta find out." Lauren's eyes

opened as I lifted her out of the truck. "Hey there, kiddo." I lowered her feet to the ground and smiled. "We're here."

Her eyes widened as she looked around. When she spotted the high metal fences with barbed wire and tall electric gate, she probably thought she'd traded one prison for another. "What is this place?"

"It's just our clubhouse. Don't worry, you're safe here." I reached for her little hand, and it trembled nervously in mine as I led her towards the back door. "Come on. We've got some friends we'd like you to meet."

Looking at her now, I was glad Stitch suggested that we help her clean off all that makeup and get her some new clothes on the way home. With her new hoodie and sweatpants, she actually looked like your typical teenager instead of some cracked-out kid prostitute. I opened the door and found Cotton and Cass waiting for us when we stepped inside. I didn't miss the disapproving look on Cotton's face as we approached them. "Like you two to meet Lauren."

"Hi there, Lauren. I'm Cass." Cass's face lit up with a bright smile as she turned towards Cotton. "And you can call him Cotton."

"Hi, Cass. Hi, Cotton. Nice to meet you," Lauren answered softly.

"I just made some pancakes. Are you hungry?" Lauren gave her a little nod, so Cass stood up and motioned for her to follow. "Come on to the kitchen and

I'll get you fixed up."

As soon as they were gone, Cotton turned to us and asked, "So, that's the kid from the auction?"

"She is," Stitch answered.

"Fuck. She's like eleven or twelve."

"The whole thing was fucked up, Prez. You wouldn't have believed it unless you saw it."

Cotton reached for a beer and then turned to me. "Got any idea what the hell we are going to do with her?"

"We gotta find out what the deal is with her folks. When I mentioned taking her home, she freaked out. Need to know why. Thought Cass might help me talk to her so we can find out what's going on."

"Don't need to waste any time with this, Mike. She's just a kid. No business being here without someone to look after her."

"I'll go talk with them now. I'll let you know what I find out." I stood and started towards the kitchen.

Before I walked out, Cotton called out to me. "You guys did good. Glad you made it back."

I nodded as I continued towards the kitchen. When I walked in, Cass and Lauren were sitting alone at the table. Lauren was trying to eat, but her trembling hands were making it difficult. It was then I realized I wasn't dealing with a case of nerves. Like Tristen, she was suffering from withdrawals. Cass's eyes were filled with concern as she said, "She's been telling me about Tristen. Did you know they were in the same room together?"

"I had no idea."

Lauren looked up at me and my heart broke when I saw the tears in her eyes. "I really wish she was here with me."

"You'll see her again, sweetheart." Cass looked down at Lauren's trembling hands and shook her head. "We need to call Doc so he can make sure she's okay."

"She's about to start having withdrawals, Cass. The shakes are just the beginning. Not sure how much help Doc's gonna be."

"If he can't help, then he'll know someone who can."

I reached for my phone and sent him a message. Once he responded, I told her, "He'll be up in a few minutes."

"Good." Cass looked back at Lauren. "Can I get you anything else?"

When she shook her head no, I said, "I need to ask you a few questions. You good with that?" She nodded, letting me know it was okay, so I continued. "Where are your folks?"

Panic filled her eyes as she looked over at Cass. Seeing that she was freaking out, Cass put her hand on her lap and said, "It's okay, sweetie. Big Mike is one of the good guys. You can trust him."

She hesitated as she looked back at me. "They're back in California. We moved there a couple of years ago when my dad lost his job."

"Can you tell me their names and their address?"

"Please… don't make me go back there. *Please*."

"No one is gonna make you go back there, Lauren. I just need to know what we're dealing with. We can't have any loose ends."

"Okay." Her eyes dropped to her lap. "My Dad's name is… Robert Baker. Mom's name is Debra."

There was something about that name that seemed oddly familiar, but I just couldn't place it. "Okay. That's good. What about your address?"

"We were living on Pine Street in Sunnybrook, California, but I doubt they still live there."

"Why? How long have you been gone?"

She fiddled with her fingernails as she answered, "A week, I guess. Maybe two. We move around a lot, so they've probably already left."

"Why's that?"

After she took in a deep breath, she looked up at me with a frustrated look. "My parents aren't good people, Mr. Mike. They're never home, and when they are, they're completely smashed. Mom told me that dad got into some trouble with this man he worked for. She said he came up short on one of his deliveries and owed some people some money. The next day, he told me I was going to go stay with my Aunt Claudia for a while. I believed him until I heard him talking to his friends. He was bragging about all this money he was gonna make and how much better their life was going to be once I was gone."

"Damn." Seeing the turmoil etched on her face, dark and full of sadness, made it impossible not to feel sorry for the kid. I'd heard of some pretty shitty parents. Hell, mine weren't the fucking Cleavers, but hers might've taken the cake. Selling their own kid to pay off a fucking debt was incomprehensible.

"Please don't send me back there," she pleaded. Her face was growing paler by the minute and her tremors seemed to be getting worse. "I can't go back."

I leaned towards her and placed my hand on her shoulder. "We'll figure something out, but for now, you need to get some rest. Gonna have a friend of mine check you out and make sure you're okay."

She brought her hand up to her head as she mumbled, "Okay… I'm not feeling so good."

Cass stood up and helped Lauren to her feet. "Let's go to Tristen's room. You can lay down there until Doc comes."

Before they left the room, I called out to Lauren. "I'll come check on you in a bit. Doc will get you fixed up."

"Thanks, Mr. Mike."

Once they were gone, I headed back to my room and sat down at my computer. Thinking it was time to do some research on Lauren's folks, I pulled up Robert Baker's rap sheet. As soon as I saw those beady eyes staring back at me, I was thrown back in time. I was back in that bathroom in juvenile hall, surrounded by Baker and his pack of wolves. The fear and the shame

I'd felt for being so weak and afraid flooded my mind. As a kid, Baker was an asshole, and after all these years, nothing had changed. He was still a fucking asshole, and I couldn't help but feel sorry for Lauren. She'd been telling us the truth when she said her parents weren't good people, but that was taking it lightly; they'd both been in and out of jail more times than I could count, locked up for something all the fucking time for all kinds of dumb shit, from DUIs and public intoxication to armed burglary and drug distribution. Over the past three years, their address changed from one dump to the next. Poor kid didn't stand a chance with either of them.

The longer I looked at Baker's face, the angrier I became. Rage crept down my neck and radiated into my hands as they curled into fists. Before I realized what I was doing, I found myself hacking into his bank account. After I wiped it out, I opened a new account in Lauren's name and deposited all the money into hers. That was just the beginning. I cut their power, their phones, and maxed out all their credit cards, leaving them both flat broke. By looking up his criminal record and his statements, I found the name of the drug dealer Baker had been caught dealing for. I hacked into his dealer's bank account and transferred all his money into Baker's, making sure to leave a trail straight to him. A move like that would have Baker's head on the chopping block, so it was only a matter of time before he'd find his end. I could've spent all day fucking with him, but Cotton was expecting me to come up with a place for Lauren to go.

I was running out of options when Maverick walked in. "Having any luck?"

I looked over at him and shook my head. "Nothing so far. From what I can tell, the poor kid's got nobody."

"Cass was pretty shaken up by some of things she told her."

"Yeah, it's pretty fucked up that a kid her age has been through the things she has."

"Maybe Doc can help her get through some of this stuff."

Remembering everything Nitro had said about Tristen, I knew it was going to be a difficult time for Lauren, especially with everything that had happened with her folks. "Thinking it isn't gonna be that easy, brother. She's gonna need some real help after all she's been through."

"Then, we'll get it for her."

I ran my hand through my hair with frustration. "What the hell are we going to do with a young girl? She can't just live at the club."

"We'll figure something out. That's what we do," Maverick assured me. "For now, we gotta focus on getting her through the next few days. The rest will come with time."

Chapter 18

Josie

It'd just been a little over a week and Tristen was already looking more like herself. I knew it had everything to do with Nitro and the rehabilitation center he'd chosen for her. It wasn't exactly conventional, but that's what I liked about it. Nitro and I were able to stay on the same premises with Tristen, so after she'd gone through their detox program, I could actually spend time with her. She was getting stronger each day, but the endless nightmares and terrifying memories were still getting to her. Thankfully, the counseling and group therapy seemed to be helping. The sessions lasted for hours, morning and afternoon, and while sometimes they were exhausting, I could tell it helped her to have someone to talk to. Each day she was getting better, which meant we were getting closer to going home.

While Tristen was in her sessions, I spent my time reading by the pool or catching up on my classwork for school. I was way behind, but thankfully, I'd been able to work it out with my professors to complete my last few projects online. Once I'd finished my latest assignment, I went to check in with Nitro. Like most days, he wasn't hard to find. He'd claimed a small corner in the lobby where he spent most of his day working. When I walked up, he was sitting at the table, talking on his phone.

"Doing better." He nodded silently as he listened to the other end of the line. He was wearing his casual clothes, dark jeans, and basic white t-shirt with just a hint of cologne. The sun reflected off his fancy, platinum watch as he held the phone up to his ear. "Gonna be here as long as it takes, brother. Got no other answer for you." He clenched his fist at his side. "I understand that, but it doesn't change anything." He glanced over in my direction, and when he saw me sitting down across from him, he turned his head and mumbled something I couldn't quite understand. After he finally hung up the phone, he cleared his throat and looked over at me. "How is she this morning?"

I wanted to ask who he was just talking to, wondering if it might've been Mike, but I decided to just let it go, knowing he wouldn't tell me either way. "Pretty good actually. She just left for her group session."

"Good to hear." He turned his attention back to his laptop, and I couldn't help but wonder what he was really doing. There were three cell phones sprawled out on the table, along with his newspaper and one of the most expensive laptops on the market. It was clear the man made a ton of money. He'd made no attempt to hide it, but after all this time, he'd never given me any clue how he'd made his fortune. I'd tried to figure it out on my own, thinking maybe he sold organs on the black market or he was some kind of drug smuggler. While I had no idea what he was into, my instincts told me it was something illegal. He was too secretive for it to be anything legit.

Unable to fight my curiosity, I asked, "What exactly do you do, Nitro?"

"What do I do?" He knew exactly what I was asking, but he was playing coy with me.

"You know… for a living?"

He thought for a moment, then answered, "I deal with supply and demand."

"Mmm-hmm. So, this supply… is it something valuable?"

"To some."

"And you are the go-to guy for this so-called supply?"

"You could say that."

His vague responses were getting under my skin. "And how does my sister fit into all this?"

"She doesn't," he answered flatly.

I sighed with frustration. "None of this makes any sense to me, Nitro, and I've gotta admit, the whole thing with the auction, and everything you're doing here with Tristen, makes me a little nervous."

"Doesn't have to make sense, Josie. Just know I'm doing this for your sister so she can have the life she deserves."

"But why?" I leaned towards him, hoping he'd give me a real answer. "I need to know what is going on in that head of yours."

"No one needs to know what's going on in this head. It's not a pretty picture, but I'll tell you this... I learned a long time ago that my gut is never wrong about *anything*. When I saw your sister standing in that auction, I knew she was scared out of her mind, but I didn't see fear or the effects of the drugs... I saw Tristen: a girl full of fight and a powerful will to survive. Every instinct I had told me to hold onto her and protect her, and that's what I'm gonna do."

"But you don't even know her."

"I know enough."

"You do realize how crazy all this sounds."

He gave me a little shrug. "I guess it does."

"I want to think you're really thinking of my sister with all of this, but part of me thinks this is more about you than her."

"Maybe."

"So, what happens when she gets better?"

"No way to know what the future holds. Only time will tell. For now, we'll just have to wait and see how everything turns out."

"Mmm-hmm." I found myself wondering how Mike and the other brothers felt about how Nitro was dealing with Tristen. I knew the club was one of those things Big told me not to ask about, but he wasn't there to stop me. "What about the club? Any idea what the future holds for you with them?"

He gave me a disapproving look, letting me know I was pushing it. "Been dealing with Cotton for a long time. Know him well enough to know he's gonna be pissed about the way I handled things. That's on me, and I'll have to deal with the blow back. I think in time, he'll understand why I made the move I did."

"Not sure that's gonna happen."

"Maybe not. Won't know until we have a face to face."

While I still wasn't sure about Nitro and why he was helping my sister, I did know that being at the rehabilitation center was helping her. "She really is doing better. He'll see that."

"Maybe." He reached for his newspaper as he asked, "You two got any plans for the afternoon?"

"Other than the same thing we did yesterday, and the day before that, and the day before that… nope. No big plans."

"Thought you could take Tristen over to the spa thing after her appointment."

"Really? That would be wonderful."

"Good. I'll get it set up."

I shouldn't have been surprised by Nitro's thoughtfulness, not after all he'd already done, but I was surprised nonetheless. Overcome with gratitude, I walked over to him and wrapped my arms around his neck, giving him a tight squeeze. "Thank you, Nitro. I still don't understand all this, but I do appreciate all you've done."

Before he had a chance to respond, I released him and headed upstairs to find Tristen. When I told her about going to the spa, she couldn't have been more excited. As I'd hoped, it was a perfect day—not because of all the pampering, but because I was able to see my sister laugh and actually enjoy herself. For just a little while, she was able to forget about all the hell she'd been through and just be happy.

"Your hair looks amazing." I'd always loved my sister's long, blonde hair, but the dark, almost black curls around her face brought out the blue in her eyes.

She played with a few strands of her hair as she stared into the mirror. "You don't think it's too much?"

"I think it's perfect." I walked up behind her and glanced at my reflection. "Mine, on the other hand, might be too much."

She turned around with her eyebrows furrowed and fussed, "It is not! I love the highlights. They go perfect with that tan you're getting. You'll be turning heads for miles."

Unfortunately, there was only one head I cared about, and it was all the way back in Washington. I'd tried to block him from my mind, but every time I turned around, he'd managed to inch his way back into my thoughts. There were times when I'd find myself smiling over something he'd said or done, while others times, I would want to claw his eyes out for making me fall for him. I blamed him totally for my broken heart. He didn't have to be so sweet, so handsome, or so damn irresistible.

I felt Tristen nudge me with her elbow. "What?"

Big

She pointed her finger at me and twirled it in the air as she asked, "You wanna tell me where your mind just went?"

"Nowhere… I was just thinking about how great your hair looks."

"Liar." She walked over to the sofa, and as she sat down, she patted the cushion beside her. "Get over here and spill it."

"There's nothing to spill, Tris." I walked over and sat down next to her. "I'm fine."

"You don't have to do that, Josie. You can talk to me."

"I know I can *talk to you*." I'd already told her about going to the club to find her, how I'd met everyone, and even told her about Stitch torturing me. But I hadn't told her exactly how I felt about Big. I couldn't. It hurt too much to think about it, much less talk about it. "I just don't see the point."

"The point is… I'm your sister, and I want to know what is going on with you." She gave me one of her looks as she asked, "Does this have anything to do with you and Big?"

"Maybe." Like a pouting child, I fell back against the sofa and crossed my arms with a huff. "I thought there might be something between us, but I was wrong. So, there ya go. That's what's going on with me."

"What makes you think you're wrong?"

"I don't know. Maybe because one minute he was acting like he was all into me, and then… poof…

nothing." I knew I was being unreasonable. Mike knew I didn't want to leave my sister, especially when I'd just gotten her back, so he encouraged me to go with her. It was the right thing to do, but he could've acted like he actually cared. He seemed completely unfazed by the fact that I was leaving, making me think I'd been wrong about everything. "He hasn't even tried to call."

"*Josie*," she scolded. "You aren't exactly being fair. Have you tried seeing his side of things?"

"I know, but…"

"Have you tried calling *him*?"

"No."

"Then call *him*."

"That's not going to happen. No way, no how."

She shook her head as she looked up at the ceiling. "You have always been such a stubborn ass, Josie Carmichael."

"I'm just not going to go chasing after some guy that obviously doesn't give two shits about me."

"Stubborn as the day is long," she scolded.

"I don't know what you expect me to do here, Tristen."

"It's time for you to decide what you really want. It's obvious that you have a thing for him, otherwise you wouldn't still be thinking about him."

"I wouldn't say *that*," I scoffed, trying to make light of my feelings.

"You know I can tell when he's on your mind. Your whole face lights up, and your cheeks get all flushed… just like they are now."

"Whatever."

"You're in *love with* him."

"I haven't really known him all that long."

"Doesn't matter how long you've known him. You're in love with him. The rest doesn't matter."

I knew it was crazy, but she was right. I did love him—more than I ever thought possible. After my parents died, I kept my guard up. I never let anyone in, no matter how great the guy, but in just a few short days, he managed to break through my walls and made me feel things that I never expected to feel. "So, what if I am?"

"Then, you have to do something about it."

"Like what?"

"Like *go* after him! Stake your claim, woman." She laughed, but I knew from the look in her eye she was being serious.

I mocked, "Stake my claim? Seriously?"

"With some guys, you have to dig around to find the good in them, if you find it at all, but it isn't like that with Big. He's got a good heart, and he's loyal and kind… and dear lord, the man is incredibly hot. If you know in your heart he's the one for you, then you have to go to him."

"And what if he doesn't feel the same about me."

"No way that would happen. Big is smart enough to know a good thing when he sees it."

"Maybe, but…"

"But *nothing*. You need to pack your bag and go get your man."

"It's not that simple. He's hundreds of miles away, and you're here. I can't just up and leave."

"You don't have to keep doing this, Josie. I'm not the same stupid kid I was when Mom and Dad died. You don't have to keep worrying about me. I'm okay. I've been okay for a long time."

"I don't mean to state the obvious here, but you were just kidnapped and almost—"

"You're right, but I'm here now. And I'm doing just fine." She walked over to me and reached for my hand. "You can't keep worrying about me all the time, Josie. You've been doing it for years. You can't focus on your own life when you're always obsessing over mine. I may not always make the best choices, but good or bad, they are mine to make. It's time for you to let go of the guilt and move on."

"You were so mad at me when I left for school. I thought you'd never forgive me."

"I was mad at the world, Josie. I had a huge chip on my shoulder, and I took it out on everyone I cared about. That's what teenagers do," she laughed. "But, I'm not a teenager anymore. I've gotten past all that, and yeah, I know my life is far from perfect, but I think I'm doing alright."

"I think you're doing better than alright."

"I am, so there's nothing holding you here. You need to get your butt in gear and go pack your bags. It's time for you to go get your man."

"My man?" I laughed. "I don't even know how he really feels about me."

"Do we need to go back over this again?" She shook her head and held up her finger. "First, he moved Heaven and Earth to get your sister back safe and sound."

"That wasn't because of me. He would've done that anyway."

"Exactly. He's good like that." She smiled as she held up a second finger. "You said he acted jealous when he saw you in that bikini. He wouldn't care if he didn't have a thing for you."

"He was being protective."

"He was being possessive. That's what men do when they want to claim a woman." She cocked her eyebrow when she held up her third finger. "He took you out to Smokey's place." Her fourth finger popped up as she continued, "He took you out on his bike. That's a big deal whether you realize it or not."

"It was just a ride."

"It's never just a ride, Josie. Never." Now, her entire hand was spread wide with all five fingers in my face. "He makes you smile and gets you all hot and bothered. If he wasn't into you, you'd see that he was just trying to get into your pants, and he wouldn't have that kind of effect on you."

"Okay, fine. You can stop already."

"Then, you're going?"

"Maybe... I'll think about it."

"See? Stubborn as the day is long."

Chapter 19

Patience was never one of my strong suits. I'd always been one to act, not stand by and wait, so trying to endure the past two weeks hadn't been easy. I'd done my best to keep my mind occupied, knowing I had to give Josie time with her sister, but I couldn't get her out of my head. Every time I closed my eyes, I'd see those beautiful eyes staring back at me. I could almost feel the curves of her body on my fingertips. Everything about her—the seductive scent of her skin, the warmth of her lips on mine, her little whimpers and moans when we made love—it was all just too much. I felt like some kind of caveman as I fought the urge to go to her, throw her over my shoulder, and bring her ass back home. As much as I wanted to do just that, I couldn't. She needed time with her sister, time to heal the wounds of the present and past, and I had to give her that. For the time being, I had to keep my mind occupied and keep the caveman in me at bay.

Thankfully, keeping busy hadn't been difficult. Between Lauren and working on our next shipment, I hadn't had much down time. With Doc's help, we'd gotten Lauren through the worst of the withdrawals. He knew someone at the Teen Drug Rehabilitation Center in Sequim, and after he explained Lauren's situation, they were willing to work with her through their outpatient program. Cass volunteered to take her to all the sessions, and she even managed to talk Cotton into letting Lauren stay with them. He was a little resistant at first, but it didn't take long for Lauren to win Cotton over. She's a great kid. She was one of those quiet, shy types, but when you finally managed to get her talking, she'd carry on for hours. Nothing beat seeing her smile, and seeing that she was adjusting so well only made us more certain that we'd made the right choice to keep her with us.

While Cass and Henley took Lauren to her morning session, I'd been working on my bike in the garage. Lunchtime came around, so I headed to the kitchen for something to eat. When I walked in, I found Wyatt and Dusty digging around in the freezer. "You lose something?"

Wyatt turned back and looked at me with surprise. "Oh, hey Big. We're looking for the ice cream."

I walked over, reached behind all the frozen vegetables, and pulled out the large tub of chocolate ice cream. "You mean this?"

"Thanks, Big." Dusty gave me one of his big grins as he took the container from my hands. "You want some?"

"No thanks, buddy. I'm going to get some lunch first." I opened the fridge, pulled out the lasagna Cass made the night before, and got myself a large helping. I was about to put it in the microwave when I noticed the boys were fixing three bowls of ice cream instead of two. "Who's that one for?"

"Lauren. She's been playing my new game with us," Wyatt explained. "She's really good at it."

"Better than me?" I teased.

He didn't bat an eye as he answered, "*Way better*."

Dusty scooped out another spoonful of ice cream and put it in the bowl. "She won the last game, so we are bringing her ice cream."

"That's nice of you." Something told me there was more to the story, but the microwave chimed with my lasagna, and I was too hungry to ask.

By the time I sat down to eat, the boys were already gone. I looked over and shook my head when I noticed the mess they'd left on the counter—drawers were left askew, the cabinets were still sitting wide open, and the carton of ice cream was on the counter melting. Before it ruined, I got up to put it away, and just as I stuck it back in the freezer, Cass walked in with Henley. "There he is."

"What's up ladies?" I asked as I walked back over to the table and sat down.

Henley came over and sat down next to me, while Cass hovered behind me.

Cass's voice was rushed and full of concern. "It's Lauren."

"What about Lauren?"

"We've got to get her into school or she'll fall behind. But we can't exactly enroll her without her birth certificate and I don't know how to get her records from her other schools. I don't even know what grade she should be in or what kind of grades she had. She might've been struggling or failing, or she could've been a straight A student, but…"

"Cass," I interrupted. "Slow down."

"I'm sorry. I get a little excited when I'm worried." She inhaled a deep breath, then continued. "When I talked to Cotton about it, he told me to come to you… Can you help?"

I knew Cass had grown attached to Lauren. You could see it in her eyes whenever she talked about her. She was so busy making sure she felt comfortable and wanted that she didn't realize how attached she'd become. "I'll take care of it."

"Are you sure you can get everything she needs?"

"I'll handle it. Just give me a couple of days."

A relieved smile crossed her face as she sat down at the table. Henley rolled her eyes as she looked over at Cass. "I told you he could do it."

"I knew he could do it, too," Cass huffed.

"Then, why the freak out?"

"Because I want all of this to work out, Henley. She's such a great kid, and she's been through so much."

"I know she has, but she's doing great."

"I hope so. I kind of like having her around." Cass smiled. "She's such an awesome kid." She looked at me. "Have you heard any more from Nitro? How's

Tristen?"

"He said she's doing good. Might be coming home in the next week or so."

"So, he's going to let her come back here?" Henley questioned.

"Can't answer that. I guess that will be up to her."

Henley got a curious look on her face as she turned to look at me. "What about Josie?"

"What about her?"

"Come on, Big. You know what I mean," Henley pushed. "We all know there was something going on with the two of you."

"*Henley*," Cass scolded.

"What?" She shrugged and continued. "It was totally obvious, Cass. They were into each other, and who could blame them? They're like the perfect match. They're both strangely smart with all that computer stuff, and they made a great team when it came to finding Tristen. Then there's the way they were always ogling each other."

"Ogling?"

"You were *so* ogling her all the time, Big. You couldn't take your eyes off her, and she was the same way about you."

"She's with her sister."

"I get that, but it's been weeks. When is she coming back? Is she coming back?"

"Guess time will tell."

"Seriously?" Henley fussed. "You aren't going to

go out there and sweep her off her feet?"

Cass gave her sister a disapproving look as she said, "Henley, leave the man alone. He knows how to handle his woman. Besides, Josie is a smart girl. She knows Big isn't the kind of guy you let slip away."

Before either of them could continue, I got up and put my plate in the sink. I had to finish some things up before I started working on Lauren's paperwork. As I headed out to the garage, I told them, "I'll get Lauren's stuff to you as soon as I can."

"Thanks, Mike. You're a sweetheart."

By the time I got back out to my bike, most of the guys had gone out on a run, leaving the garage to me and Q'. Where he was just getting started installing new chrome exhaust pipes on his bike, I was almost done installing the new sound system on mine. I just had a few final touches that I planned to get done before the end of the day. I'd been working for almost an hour and was just about to finish things up when Cotton walked into the garage. "You talk to Cass?"

"I did. I'll get in touch with my guy this afternoon. Figure he'll be able to get what we need by morning."

"Good. Don't want her getting any further behind."

"Things going okay with that? I mean… with her being out at your place?"

Cotton had always been a compassionate leader, one who we've all learned we could trust with our lives, and it was rare that he showed any sign of softness, except for when it came to Cass. She'd been the only one who'd ever been able to get to him, but I could see from the look on his face that he was warming up to Lauren. I couldn't exactly blame him. The kid was easy to get attached to, and knowing how hard she'd had it made us all want to give her a better chance at life. "I'd say things are going pretty good. She seems to be adjusting."

"And you? Are you adjusting to a house full of women?" I chuckled.

"Not sure I'll ever get used to that. Mornings are hell, brother," he complained. "I'm going to go check with Maverick. They should be heading back from Seattle by now. Let me know when you get Lauren's stuff taken care of."

"Will do."

Once he was gone, I headed back into the clubhouse with the intention of getting started on Lauren's paperwork. Since I was done with my bike, I needed a distraction. My talk with Cass and Henley had my mind on Josie, and thinking about her was the last thing I needed to do, not when my willpower was running so low. I couldn't stop wondering how she was doing. When I'd asked Nitro about her the day before, he was vague at best. The entire thing was fucking with my head, and I was finding it harder and harder to focus on anything.

Trying to shake her from my thoughts, I stopped by the bar for a drink. After grabbing a beer from the cooler, I made a call to my contact, letting him know exactly what we'd need to get Lauren enrolled in school. He'd assured me that he'd take care of it, and we should have everything we needed by morning. I tried to clear my mind and enjoy a moment alone, but the silence was just too much.

I decided to go back to my office, thinking I could keep myself busy by looking up Lauren's records from her previous schools. I'd just stepped in my office when I noticed a mountain of wrapped treats scattered all over my computer keyboard. It took my mind a minute to register what I was seeing, so I picked one up and held it in my hand, feeling the crinkle of the plastic packaging against my hand. As I looked at the trademark blue and yellow circle on the packaging, my mind went straight to Josie. She's the only one who would've put a stack of fucking MoonPies on my desk. I turned and looked around my empty room, thinking maybe she was still there. Unfortunately, there was no sign of her.

Hoping I might be able to catch her before she left, I rushed out the door and headed for the parking lot. When I walked past Tristen's room, I noticed that the door was ajar and the lights were on. Stopping dead in my tracks, I turned back and looked inside. Relief rushed over me when I caught a glimpse of Josie. I opened the door further and found her standing beside Tristen's dresser with a large duffle bag beside her feet. Like usual, she was wearing a pair of jeans with a long sleeve t-shirt, but she'd changed her hair – added highlights and maybe got a new cut – and her skin had a sun-kissed glow. I don't think I've ever seen her look more beautiful. "Josie?"

Looking totally unfazed to see me, she peered over her shoulder and smiled. "Oh. Hey, Mike."

"What the hell are you doing here?"

"It's nice to see you too, Mike." Ignoring my question, she started rummaging through the dresser drawer.

I took a step closer, trying my damnedest not to lose it, and asked her again, "*What are you doing*?"

After closing the drawer, she turned around to face me. She crossed her arms and looked at me with her eyebrows furrowed. "I came back."

"I see that."

"Okay. So, now that we've cleared that up, I've got to finish unpacking."

"*Josie*," I growled.

"What?" She held out her hands with a shrug.

I took another step towards her, closing the distance between us. "What is all this?"

The self-assured Josie I'd always known faded as a more bashful Josie took over. She bit at her bottom lip as she considered what she was going to say next. I waited patiently, and finally got an answer I didn't expect. "I'm here to stake my claim."

An odd sensation crept through me, like a smile that overtook my entire body, and I couldn't stop myself from pushing her for more. "You gonna tell me what you mean by that?"

"Do I have to?" she asked as her face flushed with embarrassment.

"You do."

"Okay, fine." She tucked a loose strand of her hair behind her ear and straightened her stance as she looked down at the MoonPie I had in my hand. "Like I told you… you're my something-good that came from something bad. You're my MoonPie, and I don't want to lose you."

"You're not going to lose me, Josie."

"I'm not taking any chances. I don't know about you, but I've never felt like this about anyone. It freaks me out a little, but I like it… a lot." Her eyes locked on mine, and I felt my blood rush through my veins as she said, "I want you, Mike. So, I'm here to stake my claim."

Fuck. The woman never stopped amazing me. Just seeing the look of love in her eyes was enough, but hearing her say the words sealed it for me. There was no going back. Josie was mine. "You don't have to stake your claim, doll. I've been yours since the first time I laid eyes on you. Just needed for you to realize it."

"Then, why didn't you say something? You just let me leave without saying a damn thing."

"You needed time with Tristen. You needed it just as much as she did. I wasn't about to get in the way of that."

"But, you could've called."

"It would've been a distraction you didn't need. Your mind would've been on me and not your sister."

"Well, it didn't make a difference. My mind was on you all the time."

"And mine has been on you. Hasn't been a minute that's passed that I haven't thought about you."

I wrapped my arms around her waist and pulled her against my chest. I'd missed her more than I'd even realized, and having her so close made my entire body ache for her.

Unable to wait a moment longer, I crushed her lips with mine. Her hands gripped at my waist, pulling me closer. A moan vibrated through her when she felt my hard cock pressing against her center. Her hand drifted down my hip towards my inner thigh as she ran her fingers over my dick, making me instantly harder. Her fingertips were like hot cinders as they grazed across my skin, fueling my uncontrollable need for her. I took a step forward and pressed her back against the wall. My hands dropped to her ass and lifted her as she wrapped her legs around my waist. When my cock brushed against her, she gasped and clutched at my sides.

With her cheeks and neck flushed red with desire, she looked at me and whispered, "I love you."

"Say it again."

Her eyes locked on mine as she repeated, "I *love* you."

I ran my hand across her shoulder and slowly

trailed kisses down the curve of her neck while I ground my cock back and forth against her center. "I love you too, Josie Carmichael."

Her fingers gripped my sides, gathering my t-shirt in her fingers as she pulled it over my head. She took a deep, shuddering breath as the palms of her hands roamed over my bare chest. An appraising look crossed her face as she slowly unwrapped her legs from my waist and lowered her feet to the floor. She gave me a light push, forcing me to take a step back as she dropped to her knees. With a hungry look in her eyes, her hands went for the buckle of my jeans. Moments later, they were settled below my hips and her fingers were wrapped around my cock. My head fell back as she took me into her mouth. The warmth of her mouth and the swirl of her tongue across the tip of my piercing made me throb with need.

"Fuck!" She looked up at me with hunger in her eyes as my hands dove into her hair, gripping tightly at the nape of her neck. Her fingers tightened around me as she continued to stroke up and down the length of my shaft. She took me in deep, greedy and needful, and every muscle in my body grew tense. Every flick of her tongue, every twist of her hand, every suck brought me closer to the edge. I wanted to savor the moment, enjoy every second of having my cock buried deep in her mouth, but my dick had other plans. "Love your mouth, Josie. Fucking incredible, but gonna need to be inside you... *Now*!"

Big

Her eyes never left mine as she loosened her grip on my cock and slowly stood up before me. My hands dropped to her waist as I reached for the hem of her t-shirt, carefully pulling it over her head. After I unclasped her bra, I slid it down her arms and tossed it to the floor. I lowered my mouth to her breasts as I captured one of her nipples in my mouth. A soft whimper filled the room as I ran the tip of my tongue across her sensitive flesh. While I tormented her with my mouth, her hands drifted down to the button of her jeans. Once she had them undone, she quickly lowered them and her lacy panties to the floor and kicked them to the side. She stood there completely bare and beautiful, making my dick throb with anticipation.

When I couldn't wait a moment longer, I growled, "Get on the bed."

My voice was deeper, more demanding than I'd intended, but a spark of lust flashed in her eyes, letting me know she liked it. She slowly stepped over to the edge of the bed and lowered herself onto the mattress. With her hair draped across her shoulder, she looked like an absolute angel. *My angel.* I couldn't take my eyes off her. She was everything I could ever imagine wanting, and she was *mine*.

Chapter 20

Josie

He stood over me, watching as I squirmed under the heat of his stare. Damn. I'd missed the way he looked at me, like I was something precious to him, something he'd give his life to protect. I knew then there was no turning back. I meant something to him, and I loved him, heart and soul. There was nothing I wouldn't do for him. I needed to feel the warmth of his body pressed against mine and feel the heat of his breath against my skin, so I pleaded, "Mike, please."

He reached for his jeans, and when he pulled a condom from his wallet, I shook my head, "No. You don't need it. I'm on the pill."

With that, he dropped it on the floor and lowered himself onto the bed, settling himself between my legs. I gasped when he reached for my thighs and pulled me closer to him. His hand drifted down between my legs, cupping my heat as his fingers raked across my center. "You're so fucking wet."

His breath was strained as he looked down at me with hunger in his eyes, and I knew he wanted me just as badly as I wanted him. He brushed his thickness against me, teasing me as he ground his hips against mine until I wrapped my legs around him, pulling him deep inside me. My entire body was consumed with need, making it impossible to focus on anything except the touch of his hands on my body, the soft whisper of his kiss, and the tingling sensation that surged through me whenever he shifted deeper within me.

At first his rhythm was slow, intense and demanding, but he suddenly stopped moving and whispered, "Later, I'm going to take my time with you. I'm gonna make you come *over* and *over* again." His voice was low and needful, making my entire body burn for him. "But for now, I'm going to fuck you hard and fast." He quickly pulled back before plunging deep inside me once again. "Need to feel you come undone for me." His pace continued to increase, setting my entire body on fire.

"Yes! Oh God, yes."

He pulled back and crashed into me again and again, driving me wild with every hard, deep thrust. I felt the familiar sensation of his piercing against my G spot, and a warmth started building in my lower abdomen. My fingers dug into the comforter, twisting and pulling, as my back arched off the bed. A deep growl vibrated through his chest as his fingers slipped into my hair, pulling back so he could expose my neck. His breath caressed my skin as he began nipping and sucking from the base of my ear down to my collarbone. My legs tightened around him as my hips involuntarily jolted forward, meeting his thrusts and taking him even deeper. I inhaled a labored breath as my body trembled and convulsed beneath him. Every muscle clenched around him as my orgasm took hold. He continued his relentless rhythm as my body jolted beneath him. Each thrust was more demanding than the last as he came closer to the edge. I was still floating on the high of my own release when I felt his body grow rigid. A deep groan echoed through the room as he drove deep inside me, holding still as he found his release.

My body fell limp as my legs dropped to the mattress and let out an exaggerated breath. "That was even better than I remembered."

A sexy little smirk crossed his face as he looked down at me. "Baby, I'm just getting started."

"You're gonna have to give me a minute. I can't even feel my legs."

He chuckled as he lowered himself onto the bed and pulled me over to his side. I rested my head on his shoulder and listened to the rapid beating of his heart. His arm curled around me, pulling me closer. "You're amazing, Josie Carmichael. I didn't know it was possible to love someone so much."

Hearing those words from him sent a shot straight to my heart. He'd showed me in countless ways, but he'd never actually said the words. My eyes met his as I said, "I love you, too. More every minute."

His mouth pressed against mine for a brief moment, then he turned his attention over to my bag sitting on the floor. "I hope you didn't do much unpacking."

"I've only done a little. Why?"

"Cause we're taking your stuff over to my place

later tonight. You'll be staying there, not here."

"Staying with you?"

"That's what I said." He kissed me on the temple and dropped his head back down on the pillow.

"Wait." I propped myself up on my elbow and couldn't hide my surprise as I asked, "You don't live here?"

"No, baby. I've got a place up towards Hurricane Ridge. It's just easier to stay here when we have stuff going on."

I lowered my head back down on his chest. "Okay, that makes sense, but I have an apartment of my own. Things I'll need to take care of."

"Don't sweat the small stuff. Just minor details that we'll sort later. For now, we'll get you settled at my place, and then the rest will fall into place."

He made it all sound so simple, and maybe it was. When you know it's right, you find a way to make it work. After all we'd been through, it was hard to believe that everything was really coming together so effortlessly. "Is this really happening?"

He gave me a light squeeze as he kissed me on the forehead. "Yeah, sweetheart. It's really happening, but you should know something... I'm gonna fuck this up. I'm gonna do stupid shit. Gonna say the wrong thing and piss you off. I'm gonna end up aggravating the hell out of you from time to time, but Josie, I promise you this... I will love you like no other man can. Every minute of every hour, you will know that you are mine and nothing will ever be as important to me as you are."

I looked up at him and smiled. "See... I was right. You are totally my MoonPie."

"You aren't going to give that up, are you?" He laughed.

I shrugged my shoulders and giggled. "Well, when I'm right, I'm right."

"Maybe so." He looked over at me with lust-filled eyes. "How are those legs feeling?"

A smile crept across my face as I answered, "I can feel them, if that's what you mean."

"That's what I was hoping you'd say."

He lifted me on top of him, sliding deep inside me as I straddled him. I never knew something could feel so good. I slowly started to rock my hips, and my entire body came alive. We spent the next hour making love, slow and sensual, and by the time we were done, I was just a pile of mush lying next to him.

I could've stayed there nestled up next to him for an eternity, but Mike had other ideas. He decided it was time to take me out to his place, so after a hot shower together, we got dressed and headed out into the hall. When we got to the bar, several of the guys were sitting at one of the tables having a drink while the girls were sitting at the bar. Cassidy's eyes widened with surprise when she spotted us walking through the door. "Josie?"

Henley and Wren turned excitedly at the sound of my name. It felt good to see that they were happy to see me. "Hey, guys."

Big

"I had no idea you were back. Get your butt over here."

"I'll be right back." Mike gave me a quick wink and headed over to speak to Stitch.

When I got over to the girls, Cassidy reached over the counter and gave me a quick hug. "We haven't seen you in a while. How's it going?"

"Going really good actually."

"How's Tristen?"

"The first week after we left LA was pretty rough, but things are getting a little easier for her now. She seemed really good when I left. I think she's missing you guys."

"We've missed her, too. We were really worried about her. I'm glad to hear she's doing okay."

Henley glanced over at Mike and then back to me as she whispered, "So, did you and Mr. Big Stuff get yourselves sorted?"

"We did," I answered, unable to hide my smile.

"Good. I was hoping you would." Her smile was sincere, and it meant the world to me. "Liking the new look. Your hair looks great."

I ran my fingers through my hair as I rolled my eyes. "You think so? I don't even think Mike noticed."

I hadn't even realized Mike had walked up until he placed his hands on my hips. "Oh, I noticed." Without giving me any sign of whether he liked it or not, he leaned over me and asked, "You ready?"

"Where are you two headed?"

"Taking her out to the house."

"You gonna bring her back soon so we can catch up?"

He placed his hands on my hips. "It'll have to be tomorrow. She's all mine tonight."

"Alright, then. How about lunch one day this week?" Cassidy asked.

"Sounds good to me. Just let me know when and where."

"I could do Friday," Henley chimed in. "You good with that, Wren?"

"That would be perfect. Mia is with the sitter on Fridays. Maybe we can get MJ and Allie to come along. I'll give them a call tomorrow."

"Tell them we'll go have Mexican."

My stomach churned at the thought. "Can we *not* have Mexican?"

Cassidy grimaced as she replied, "Damn. I'm sorry, girl. I wasn't even thinking. We can have whatever you want."

"How about Italian?" I suggested.

"Consider it a plan."

"Looking forward to it."

When Mike and I turned to leave, one of them yelled, "You two have fun."

"Try to behave, Henley."

By the time we got on the bike and out on the main road, the sun was starting to set. As we got farther into the mountains, it was absolutely breathtaking. I'd never seen anything so beautiful, and being on the bike made it that much better. The fresh air, the cool breeze against my face, and being so close to Mike made it a perfect drive. We hadn't been riding long when he pulled onto a long, curvy driveway that led to a ranch-style house on the side of the mountain. I'm not sure where I imagined he'd live, but this definitely wasn't what I was expecting. It was a gorgeous house painted dark gray with long white shutters and windowpanes with a wraparound porch. There were potted plants lining the steps and white chairs nestled by the front door.

He parked the bike and waited for me to get off. As I took off my helmet, I continued to look around the yard and out over the mountain. "Mike, this place is unbelievable."

"Glad you like it." He reached for my hand as he started for the steps. "But it could use a woman's touch."

He unlocked the door and motioned for me to go inside. I stepped through the door into a large living room with dark, wood floors and taupe-colored walls. It was simple and very masculine, but a few touches of color and some simple art work or flowers would be all it would take to make it perfect. The large kitchen was warm and inviting with its white cabinetry and stainless steel appliances. I took a few steps down the hall, but stopped when I walked past his office. His office at the club was impressive, but it was nothing in comparison to this. Every computer gadget known to man was crammed in that room, making me wonder why he didn't use it more often. I continued down the hall to his bedroom. It was your typical guy's bedroom with a king size bed and dark furniture. Like the rest of the house, it was simple yet elegant. I couldn't believe I'd actually be living here. "I really love it, Mike."

"You haven't seen anything, yet."

He started walking towards the back and opened a door. He motioned for me to follow him outside. When I stepped out onto the porch, the view blew me away. Even in the dark, I could see mountains for miles. It was absolutely stunning. "I don't ever want to leave from this spot."

He came up behind me, towering over me as he wrapped his arms around my waist. "I love it out here. Great place to forget your troubles."

"Do you spend a lot of time out here?"

"Not as much as I'd like to. Thinking that will change now."

"Probably so, because I'm gonna want my coffee out here every morning."

"Is that right?"

"Mmm-hmm." I nodded. "Every morning."

"And who's gonna be making this coffee for you every morning?"

"Depends on who gets up first. Something tells me that's gonna be you most days." I tried to hold back my laugh. "You do know how to make coffee, right?"

"I think I can manage, but it's gonna cost you," he

teased.

"Oh, yeah?"

"Gotta pay the toll, baby."

Knowing exactly what he meant and knowing that I would be getting just as much as him out of *that toll*, I replied, "I'm sure we can work something out."

"I'm sure we can," he chuckled.

I don't know what triggered the thought, but I found myself thinking of Tristen and Nitro. Maybe it was because I was so happy and I desperately wanted the same for my sister. I had no idea how she truly felt about Nitro. It was obvious that he felt something for her. It was written all over his face whenever he talked about her, and I couldn't help but wonder what was going to happen between the two of them. The cards were already stacked against them, and with everything that happened in LA, things were only going to get harder for them.

"I probably shouldn't ask, but what's gonna happen with the club and Nitro?"

"You're right. You shouldn't ask."

I turned around to face him and placed my hands on his chest. "I'm not asking what he does for the club or any of that. I just want to know if things are going to be okay between Nitro and the brothers. Can you tell me that?"

"Nitro will be fine with or without the club, and we will be fine without him."

"So… that's a no?"

"I don't know how things are going to play out between Nitro and Cotton. Ultimately, that's between them."

"But she's doing so much better. You should've seen that place. The counselors and the—"

"None of that matters, Josie." He could see that I was worried, so he placed his hand on my shoulder. "Things will work themselves out."

"I hope so."

"Nitro has a way of growing on you."

I shook my head and sighed. "He does, and it's frustrating as hell. I wanted to hate him, but I couldn't, not with everything he was doing for Tristen."

"Don't always agree with his methods, but he makes things happen. Gotta give him that." He reached for my hand and pulled me over to him. "You hungry?"

"Starving."

"I've got steaks we could grill, or we could go into town for something."

"I'd rather stay here if it's okay with you."

"Absolutely." He reached into his pocket for his phone. "I'll get one of the guys to bring your stuff over so you can get settled."

"That would be great."

"Make yourself comfortable while I go get dinner started." He bent down and kissed me tenderly before he turned and headed inside. I stood there for a moment, feeling in complete awe of how dramatically my life had changed in such a short time. One horrific moment in time transcended me into a life I could've only imagined. Like Nitro had once told me, there was no way to know what the future held, but for the first time since my parents died, I felt like everything was going to be okay. More than okay. Things were going to be good. Very good indeed.

Chapter 21

It had been just over a week since we'd gotten Josie's stuff moved out of her apartment and over to the house. We were already settling into our own routines. I'd make her a cup of coffee before I left for the club, and she'd take it out to the back porch to drink while she worked on her class assignments. After the day was done, I'd come home and we'd spend the night together. I'd always liked my house and tried to make it a place I could be proud of, but since she'd moved in, it felt like home. It wasn't because of the subtle changes she'd made around the house, the hot meals on the table, or even the cleaning and all the laundry. It felt like home simply because she was there. At the end of the day, it gave me a sense of peace knowing she'd be there waiting for me, just like she would be later tonight.

Knowing that later Josie was going to be at the house grilling steaks, I was eager to get my ass on my bike and out on the road, but I had a shit ton of work to finish before I could leave. I was busy getting it done when Maverick came by my office. "Cotton's called us into church."

Surprised, I stood up and followed him out into the hall. The guys made it back from the run without any issue, so I wondered why he'd call church so unexpectedly. "Something up?"

"Nitro."

We all knew it was coming. Eventually, there had to be some kind of resolution between Nitro and the club, but with the way things played out, it wasn't going to be some simple fix. I followed Maverick into the meeting room and took my seat at the table. Once everyone was settled, Cotton told us, "Got a call from Nitro. He wants to come to terms... see if we can come up with some kind of agreement."

"What kind of agreement is he looking to get?" Clutch questioned. Clutch was one of our more level-headed brothers. He liked to weigh all the options before he made any decisions, but from the angry tone in his voice, I could see he was pissed.

"That's up to us." Cotton inhaled a deep breath. "Nitro double-crossed us. There's no going back from that shit."

"As a club rule, we should put a bullet in his ass," Guardrail growled. He wasn't a man who believed in second chances. Period. "That's what happens when you fuck with the club."

I'd been there with Nitro when it had all gone down and knew firsthand just how bad it had gotten. "I don't necessarily disagree, but he did get Tristen back without causing a war between us and the fucking cartel. And he covered all the costs. He covered everything to get her back safe. That has to count for something."

Stitch leaned forward and looked at Cotton.

"Maybe so, but if we can't trust him, we sure as hell can't do business with him."

Cotton leaned back in his chair as he crossed his arms. "Been dealing with Nitro for a long time. We had a good run, but Stitch is right. Nitro violated our trust. There's no way we can continue to do business with him."

"Then, where does that leave us with our next shipment?" Guardrail asked.

"We've got other suppliers. We'll have to pool resources and make it work. That's what we do."

Knowing Josie would want to know if her sister would be back in town, I asked, "When is he coming?"

"Told him to come by this afternoon. Gonna bring Tristen with him."

Guardrail turned and asked Cotton, "And what's going to happen with her?"

"Figure that will be up to Tristen. She wasn't an ol' lady, just a hang-around. We were there for her when she needed us. It's time for her to decide where she goes from here."

"Guess we have our answer."

"We do." Cotton stood up as he said, "Meeting adjourned."

I wasn't surprised by the brothers' decision to end things with Nitro. He'd fucked up, and in the end, it had cost all of us. I just hoped it was worth it. Once everyone dispersed, I headed back to my office and messaged Josie, letting her know that Tristen was coming to the clubhouse. It'd been less than an hour after I'd messaged her when she came rushing into my office. "Is she here?"

"Not yet, but it shouldn't be much longer."

"I can't believe she didn't tell me she was coming," she pouted. "I just talked to her last night and she didn't say anything about coming home."

"Maybe she wanted to surprise you."

"Maybe, but she could've given me a hint."

I reached for her, pulling her onto my lap as I kissed her. "Not so good with surprises, are ya?"

"Well, it depends on the surprise." She leaned in and pressed her lips against mine. The kiss quickly became heated. She felt so fucking good pressed against me, and we were just about to get carried away when Stitch knocked at my door. "We've got company."

"They're here." I stood up and carefully lowered her feet to the floor. "I need you to go to Tristen's room and wait there until I come to get you."

"Why?"

"This isn't up for debate, Josie."

She looked up at me with worried eyes. "Wait... Is there going to be some kind of trouble because Nitro is coming to the clubhouse?"

I looked down at her with my eyebrow raised, letting her know I wasn't going to give her an answer. Her voice shot up several octaves when she argued, "Really? This is one of those things I'm not supposed to ask about?"

She looked so damned cute standing there with her arms crossed and that little scowl on her face. "Yep."

I heard her sigh with aggravation as she followed me out into the hall. "I really don't like that rule. Keep your mouth shut, don't ask questions. Blah, blah, blah. It's so frustrating."

"You'll manage."

"Yeah, I can manage, but it doesn't mean I'm gonna like it."

I opened Tristen's door and motioned for her to go inside. "No one said you had to like it, Josie, but as my ol' lady, it's one of the things you're gonna have to deal with."

"Your ol' lady?" Her eyes lit up as she smiled.

"You heard me. Now, get your cute ass in there and stay put until I get back."

I was about to turn to leave when she said, "You know what?"

"Hmm?"

She walked over and rose up on her tiptoes as she planted her lips against mine. "I may not like your rules, but I kind of like you."

"Kind of?"

"Yeah, but don't let it go to your head."

"I'll do what I can." I gave her a quick slap on her ass and headed out the door. "Hold tight. It shouldn't be long."

I headed down the hall towards Cotton's office, but stopped when I heard his voice coming from the bar.

Big

When I walked in, Cotton had his arms wrapped around Tristen, hugging her tightly. "Looking good, kid."

I almost didn't recognize her with her dark, wavy hair and fancy clothes. Her blue eyes filled with tears as she said, "Thank you for all you did to help me get back. I was worried I might never see this place again."

"I'm sure the girls will be glad to see you, too. Cass and Peyton are in the kitchen. Why don't you go check in with them while we have a word with Nitro?"

She hesitated as she turned back and looked at Nitro. Once he'd given her a slight nod, she turned back and answered, "Sure. It would be great to see them."

By the time she was gone, Guardrail and Maverick had come into the bar. We all gathered behind Cotton, glaring at Nitro as we waited for one of them to speak. A lesser man would've been intimidated by the show of power, but Nitro seemed unaffected as he looked at Cotton. "We've come to a crossroads, brother. I know you are set on severing ties between us, and I'm not here to change your mind."

"That's a good fucking thing, because there is nothing you could do or say that would change my mind," Cotton growled.

"Figured as much. Known you long enough to know how goddamned stubborn you can be." Nitro had balls of steel to run his mouth, but he was never one to hold back.

"Being fucking stubborn has nothing to do with it. We trusted you, and you stabbed us in the motherfucking back," Cotton shouted.

"I saved your girl from the fucking cartel, Cotton. Got her the help she needed to get back on her feet. If that's stabbing you in the back, then it is what it is."

"Don't try to turn this around, brother," Cotton roared. "You fucked this whole thing up, and you know it. Had to be the fucking hero for some girl, and to hell with the consequences."

"I had my reasons."

"Pussy isn't a fucking reason to turn your back on the club."

Nitro took a step towards Cotton and snarled, "Walking a thin line, Cotton. Truth is, you'd do the same damn thing if Cass was standing up there, being sold like a piece of fucking meat."

"I wouldn't have double-crossed the brothers."

"You're a goddamned saint, Cotton. Never had any fucking regrets. Must be nice to walk around in those fucking boots of yours." Nitro shook his head in disgust. "No sense in continuing this bullshit. What's done is done."

"Couldn't agree more." Cotton's expression was full of anger as he nodded towards the door. "Nothing keeping you here."

"If you're ready for me to go, then get Tristen back in here. Ask her yourself and see what she really wants to do. If she chooses to stay here with you and keep the life she had, then I'll walk out of here and never look back. But if she decides to go with me, then I'm taking her. Either way, this shit ends today."

Cotton turned to me and said, "Go get her."

I nodded, then turned and headed for the kitchen. When I walked in, the girls were talking a mile a minute and didn't even notice when I came through the door. "Tristen, Cotton needs you."

The chatter immediately stopped as they all turned to face me. Tristen's eyes widened with worry as she started walking towards me. "Is everything okay?"

"It's fine," I assured her. "Just need a minute."

She followed me back into the bar, and I could see that she was nervous as she walked over to Cotton. "Big said you wanted me."

"I do." He stepped closer to her and placed his hand on her shoulder, trying to comfort her as he said, "Need to know what you want to do."

"About?"

"Do you want to come back here and stay at the club... or do you want to leave here with *him*? The choice is yours, doll."

She paused for a moment as she looked over at Nitro. There was something about the way she looked at him that let me know her answer before she even said the words. Moments later, she looked back at Cotton and said, "I'll never be able to thank you for all you've done for me, Cotton. I don't know what I would've done if you hadn't let me stay here. All the guys have been good to me, and I love all of you... but, I don't belong here anymore."

"You sure about this?"

She glanced back over at Nitro and then answered, "I am. This is something I need to do."

He removed his hand from her shoulder and took a step back. "You gotta do what's right for you, Tristen. I get that. Just know the door is always open."

"Thank you, Cotton," she cried as she gave him a hug. She quickly wiped her tears away as she turned and looked at us. "I guess I better go get my stuff."

"I'll give you a hand," I offered as I followed her down to her room. I didn't mention Josie, so she was a little surprised to find her sister anxiously waiting inside when she opened the door.

"Tristen!" she shouted as she rushed over and gave her a big hug. "I can't believe you're really back! Why didn't you tell me you were coming?"

"It was a spur of the moment kind of thing. I wasn't expecting to be released until later in the week, but Dr. Jeffries said I was ready."

Josie took a step back and studied her sister for a moment. "So, you're really okay?"

"I'm more than okay, Josie." She walked over to her closet and pulled out several suitcases. "I could use some help, if you don't mind."

"What are you doing?"

"I'm packing." She walked over to her dresser and pulled everything out of the drawer, shoving it into one of the suitcases. "Can you grab the stuff out of the closet and put it in the hanger bag?"

Big

With a puzzled look, Josie asked, "Why are you packing?"

"Because I'm leaving. Nitro has arranged for me to stay in one of the lofts in his apartment building."

I could see the wheels turning as Josie stood there staring at her sister. "You're really leaving?"

"I'm moving, not leaving. I'll just be a few minutes away, and I'll have a place of my own."

"You mean a place Nitro is paying for?" Josie argued.

Tristen turned to face her sister. "He is, but not for long. I'll pay rent once I get my first paycheck."

"Paycheck? Where are you—?"

"Stop, Josie. Just stop. I know this isn't a perfect situation, but it's a fresh start. I need your support on this."

Josie took in a deep breath and sighed. She was worried, but anyone could see Tristen had come a long way over the past month. "Okay. I'll pack the clothes in the closet. Don't forget all that stuff you have in the bathroom."

I leaned against the doorframe and watched as they filled up the suitcases with her clothes, shoes, and makeup. They were just about to finish up when Nitro came up beside me. "They about got it?"

"Getting close, I think. She's got a crap-ton of stuff crammed into this little room."

"Guess I better start loading this into the truck." I followed Nitro as he took a step inside and grabbed several of the bags. The girls continued talking and packing as he walked out to the parking lot and loaded the bags into the back of his SUV. Once we were done, Nitro offered me his hand. "Thanks, brother."

"Let the dust settle, and I'll be in touch. Know Josie is gonna want to check in with her sister."

"You know my number."

Just as we got everything loaded into the truck, Tristen and Josie came outside with the last of her bags. Before Tristen got in the truck, she assured Josie once again that she was sure about leaving. "I'll call you in a couple of days. I'll come meet you for lunch or something."

She gave her a big hug, and then turned to get into the truck. Before they pulled out of the parking lot, Josie walked over to Nitro's window. When he'd rolled it down, she leaned in and said, "I'm trusting you to take care of her, Nitro. Don't let me down."

He gave her a slight nod. "You know I will."

We watched silently as they pulled out onto the main road. Once they were out of sight, Josie looked over at me. "You think she's going to be okay with him?"

"I do."

"Okay. Then I'll try to stop freaking out." She tried to feign a smile, but I wasn't buying it.

"Might want to try harder," I teased. I wrapped my arms around her, holding her close as I kissed her on the forehead. "She's going to be fine. I'll make sure of it."

Big

She sighed with relief and smiled. "How did I get so lucky?"

I'd never planned to fall in love. I never found much use in it and certainly never really thought I was any good at it, but all that changed when I met Josie. Looking at her and seeing the undeniable love in her eyes, I knew how good I had it, and I would move Heaven and Earth to hold onto it. "I'm the lucky one, Josie."

Epilogue

Four Years Later

Over the years, we'd had all kinds of cookouts and parties, but this party was like none other. The brothers and their ol' ladies had gone all out for Lauren's sweet sixteen party, and it was a perfect day for it. It was a warm, beautiful day, and they had picnic tables covering the backyard and colorful balloons spread out all over the place. There was music playing, and everyone was ready to celebrate Lauren's birthday. A pretty big crowd had gathered. Not only our kids and families, but quite a few of her friends from school were there. We all wanted to be there to spend the special day with her, especially Cotton. He was determined to make the day perfect for her. Over the years, Lauren had truly become like a daughter to him, and there was nothing he wouldn't do for her. He'd wanted to buy her a new bike, but Cass convinced him it wouldn't be practical, especially since she planned to go off to college in a couple of years. Agreeing that it wasn't an option, he bought her a bright red Volkswagen Beetle and hid it in the garage so he could surprise her when the time was right.

The brothers gathered around the grill making hot

dogs and hamburgers for the kids while the women were busy putting the food on the tables. I spotted Cotton off by himself, and he didn't look happy. When I walked up, he motioned his head towards Lauren and her friends. "You got any idea who that kid is?"

After a closer look, I realized he was talking about the tall, lanky boy who stood next to Lauren. "Nope. Never seen him."

"Don't like him."

I looked back over at the kid and saw that he was staring at Lauren, and I immediately knew exactly why Cotton wasn't happy with him. "Looks like he might have himself a crush on our girl."

"He better think twice about that shit. She's just sixteen," Cotton grumbled.

"You know, Prez... most girls start dating when they turn sixteen."

He looked over at me with an disgruntled glare. "Not my daughter. She can start dating when she goes off to college, or better yet... when she graduates from college."

Cass walked up behind him and slipped her hands around his waist. "You behaving over here?"

"Always."

"Mmm-hmm. Then can you tell me why you keep giving that poor boy the stink eye?" she teased.

"I don't know what you're talking about."

"Don't give me that, Cotton. You know good and well what I'm talking about. That poor kid is going to have a complex when he leaves here."

"So?" Cotton shrugged. "A little complex never hurt anybody."

"Stop before you freak him out more than he already is. You'll upset Lauren." Cass shook her head as she started walking back towards the others. "Hey, Big… when you get a minute, Josie needs your help with something in the kitchen."

"Alright. I'll head that way now." I glanced at Cotton and smiled. "Don't think you've gotta worry about the scrawny kid, Cotton. But the guy over by the bonfire… the one Lauren's been eyeballing since he got here. Now *he* might be a problem."

Laughing, I gave him a pat on the back and headed inside to find Josie. When I walked in, she was washing the dishes in the sink. I slipped up behind her and gave her a quick kiss just below her ear. "Hey, sweetheart. Cass said you needed help with something."

"Wow, that was fast." She reached for a towel and turned to face me as she dried her hands. She wouldn't make eye contact with me and her cheeks flushed bright red, so I knew something was up. In all the years we'd been together, she'd never been one to be able to hide anything from me. Whenever she had something on her mind, it was always written all over her face. Trying to be nonchalant, she looked at me and smiled. "Hey."

"Hey, baby. You okay?"

"Yep. I'm fine." She was lying.

"So, what did you need help with?"

Big

She bit her bottom lip as she pointed at the cabinet next to her. "I… uh... I need you to get a box down for me. It's on the top shelf and I can't seem to reach it."

"Yeah, I can do that." Knowing that she was up to no good, I opened the cabinet door and was caught off-guard when I saw a box of mini MoonPies sitting on the top shelf. I reached for them and asked, "Is this what you were needing?"

"Yep, that's it." Still trying to act like it was no big deal, she handed me a bowl. "I need to take them outside. Can you put them in this for me?"

I had no idea what she was up to, but she was so damned cute that it was hard not to play along. "Sure thing."

I opened the box and turned the box upside down. All the little packages came pouring out at once. I wasn't catching on to the game she was playing until a small slip of paper landed in the bowl. I reached for it with curiosity. "What's this?"

"Flip it over."

When I turned the page over, it was a photograph of an ultrasound. I looked closer and noticed Josie's name at the top. In half a daze, I stood there staring at the tiny blob on the photograph. It took several seconds for it all to sink in. "Is this what I think it is?"

"It's our own little MoonPie, Mike." She smiled nervously. "I went to the doctor this morning, and she told me I'm about eight weeks along."

My chest tightened as I looked at my wife, knowing

that I was the luckiest man on the planet. She was simply amazing. She faced things head on, never giving up on the things that were important to her. I couldn't fathom what my life would've been like without her. She was my world, my everything, and now she was having a kid. "How?"

"Do I really need to explain that to you?" She stepped closer to me and looked down at the picture in my hand. "I was feeling a little off, especially in the morning, so I went in to see the doctor. She did a few tests, and that's when she told me I was pregnant."

I had a million things I wanted to say to her, but the words were trapped in my throat. I couldn't have been happier, but she mistook my silence as ambivalence.

"I know we were planning to wait because of work and all, but my due date is around April." After she'd graduated, she'd gotten a job at the high school teaching computer programing. Her job was important to her, and she'd wanted to hold off on kids until she'd gotten a few years under her. "But, summer break will be just around the corner, so I'll only miss a few weeks of school. I think it'll be okay."

"It'll be more than okay, Josie." I wrapped my arms around her, pulling her close as I said, "It'll be incredible. I've just got one request."

Her eyebrows furrowed as she cocked her head to the side. "What's that?"

"We're not naming this kid MoonPie or Moon or Pie, or anything in between."

"I'm good with that," she chuckled.

"And I'm good with you. I love you, Josie Davis." I kissed her softly on the temple.

"And I love you." She placed her hands on my chest and smiled. "You know we'll probably have to change your office into the nursery."

"My office?"

"I know you love it and all, but it's really the only place that will work."

"Josie."

"Hmm?"

"You gotta know, there's nothing in this world I wouldn't do for you."

She smiled as she said, "Well, technically it isn't for me."

"Okay, then let me clear this up for you." I placed the palm of my hand on her stomach as I said, "There's nothing in the world I wouldn't do for you or our kid. The two of you are everything to me."

I leaned down and kissed her once again. In just a few brief moments, she'd changed my life once again, making me happier than I ever dreamed possible. She'd been right when she said good things come from bad ideas, because nothing could've been better than having her in my arms.

The End.
More from the Satan's Fury Series coming soon.

Acknowledgements

MJ at Mayhem Cover Creations – Thank you for making such awesome covers. You always do such an amazing job. If you need a great cover, be sure to reach out to MJ. She's awesome! mayhemcovercreations.com

Amanda Faulkner – I can't thank you enough. Not only are you an amazing PA, you are truly a wonderful friend. Thank you for being such an awesome PA. I couldn't do it without you. Love ya.

Natalie Weston – Thank you being such a huge support. Your kind words and encouragement keep me going. I'd be lost without you. Your positive attitude is contagious. Don't ever lose it.

Daryl and Sue Banner, The Dynamic Duo – Thank you both for all your hard work and for putting up with all of my craziness. I don't know how you do it! I truly appreciate your dedication to making my book the best it can be.

* If you haven't checked out Daryl Banner's books on Amazon, you are missing out. Be sure to check out his books: www.amazon.com/author/darylbanner

Big

Tempting Illustrations – Thank you for your amazing teasers. I loved them all! If you're looking for some amazing teasers, be sure to check them out. http://www.temptingillustrations.com

Danielle Palumbo – You are officially my Wonder Woman. I can't thank you enough for all you do. Your support and help with the book means more to me than you will ever know. Thank you for being you.

Demetra Toula Illiopoulos- Thank you so much for all of your support and your friendship. It means more than you know.

Neringa Neringiukas – You're amazing. Thank you for your suggestions and all your amazing reviews. I can't thank you enough for sharing my book and teasers, and all your kind words of support. You rock!

Ana Rosso – My young Jedi. Thank you for keeping me on track, even when life tends to get in the way. I am so proud of you for writing your first book, Reaper's Creed MC. I can't wait to see what you come up with next. Keep writing!!
https://www.amazon.com/Reapers-Creed-MCDamons-Salvation-ebook/dp/B01HG1G6PS

Patricia Ann Blevins, Kaci Stewart, , Tanya Skaggs, Terra Oenning, Sarah Hooks, Sabra Browning Barowski (loved all your messages! Thanks for checking out the rest of the series), Stacie Lee, Casey Bedolla, Jennifer Yarbrough, Gina Dickerson, Stephanie Page, Jacey Jeffrey, Sunny Harley, Amanda Evans, Bille Jean Ashworth, Martha Lanham, Kaci Stewart, Jennifer Davidson, Courtney Cartman, Jessica Blank, Dana Kimberly, Tawnya Huffman, Jaclyn Ryan, Grace Hart, Sarah Harmon, Hannah, Myers, Samantha Ortegon, Ann Tracy, Jenn Allen, Kat Beecham, Rory Lampley, Lisa Cullinan, Gloria Esau, Michelle Shelly, Melanie DeVotie, Katie Nuzzi Gittel, Charolette Smith, Melissa Smith, Race Crespin, Michelle Presley, Jessica Canoto, Rachel Hadley, and Donna Parrott. – Thank you so much for always being there with your kind words and support. Your reviews and suggestions mean the world to me. Your stories and words of encouragement always make me smile. Thanks so much for sharing them with me.

Wilder's Women – I am always amazed at how much you do to help promote my books and show your support. Thank you for being a part of this journey with me. I read all of your reviews and see all of your posts, and they mean so much to me. Love you big!

Lisa Cullinan – Thank you for all your help. It's always great to have another set of eyes checking over things. I truly appreciate it. You're awesome.

Big

A Special Thanks to Mom – Thank you for always being there to read, chapter by chapter, giving me your complete support. You are such an amazing person, and I am honored to call you my mom.

Continue for an excerpt of Smokey: Book 5 in the Satan's Fury MC Series

Smokey

Satan's Fury MC
Book 5

Smokey,

I never expected this. You caught me by surprise. You stole my heart and made me feel things I never thought I could feel. I've never loved anyone the way I love you. No one. There were days when I would look at you and think it couldn't be possible for me to love you any more than I already did. Then you'd say something to make me laugh or look at me with those beautiful, blue eyes and smile, and I just couldn't help but love you even more. That's why it's so hard for me to write this letter. I can actually feel my heart breaking as I write the words, and I know after this, I will never be the same again.

I'm leaving, Smokey. By the time you read this letter, I will already be packed up and gone. We are from different worlds, traveling on two completely different paths, and in time, it would tear us apart. As much as I love you, I can't keep lying to myself. I know in my heart that leaving now is the only way to prevent that from happening. I love you. More than you will ever know. But this is how it has to be. If you ever cared about me at all, please don't try to find me. Just let me go. It's the best thing for both of us.

Love always,
MJ

Chapter 1
Smokey

It was a night like any other, or so I thought. Just like a hundred times before, I'd spent most of my night in church listening to Cotton and the brothers negotiate club business. As an officer of the club, I'd been given the job of keeping our prospects in check and determining their best use in helping with the club's biggest priorities. While negotiating the final details of our new pipeline, I had to make sure the prospects were where they needed to be and doing exactly what they were told to do. The club was embarking on new territory. For the first time, we were working with neighboring chapters of Satan's Fury to establish a shipping route that would enable us to make the biggest delivery of AK47s to date. Everything had to go exactly as planned, so we'd all have to work together to ensure there were no surprises. After going over all of the particulars, it was clear that the days ahead weren't going to be easy for any of us, especially with all the runs back and forth from here to Salt Lake and all the dealings in-between, but we'd make it happen. We always did.

As soon as we were dismissed from church, I headed straight for my bike. I hadn't eaten a bite since breakfast, so I pushed the throttle back and headed towards Mikey's Diner. It was late, so by the time I got there, it was nearly closing time and the crowd was dying down—just the way I liked it. Mikey's was an old sports bar with several large televisions lining the wall and high top tables with stools. He'd renovated the place a few years back hoping to draw in some new customers, but it didn't pan out; it was still the same old crew, drinking and eating the same thing night after night.

The alluring smell drifting from the kitchen made my stomach growl as I made my way to the back of the bar. I found a seat, and as soon as the waitress came over, I ordered beer and a burger. Once I had the beer in my hand, I took a long pull and settled back in my seat, trying my best to take a break from the mountain of thoughts that were piling up in the back of my mind. I knew it wouldn't work. Hell, it'd take a lot more than just one beer to ease any of the tension I was feeling, but I did what I could. I took a deep breath and listened to the blues playing on the jukebox. By the time I finished eating my burger, I felt a little better. Knowing the waitress was ready to call it a night, I took one last slug of my beer, laid down a twenty, then headed for the door. All I could think about was getting home, taking a hot shower, and getting some sleep.

The last thing I expected was an encounter with a beautiful stranger to completely rock my fucking world, but it did. It rocked me right to the core.

As soon as the restaurant's lights shut off, complete

darkness fell over the parking lot, making it difficult to
see as I started down the steps. As usual at this time of
night, the lot was nearly empty. There was only one car,
and it was parked next to my bike. I didn't think much
of it until I heard a woman's voice coming from behind
it, and from her tone, she didn't sound happy.

I followed the voice to the side of the car and found
a woman kneeling beside the trunk. In the darkness, I
could only make out a jumble of blonde hair and high
heels as she sat there cursing under her breath. She dug
around in her purse while I stood there watching her,
silently shaking my head as she tossed all of her
belongings onto the gravel one by one. She was
completely focused on that damn purse and had no idea
I was even standing there.

"Shit! There has to be something in here that will
open that stupid door," she growled with a slight
southern drawl. She finally gave up and tossed the bag
to the ground. She grabbed her cell phone and aimed the
flashlight towards the ground as she studied everything
that she had laid out. When the light swooped over my
boot, she gasped loudly, almost falling backwards with
shock. She quickly regained her composure and jolted
upright. She took several shaky steps back as she
pointed the blinding light from her phone towards me.
Still trying to get her footing, she shouted, "Shit! You
scared the hell out of me! What are you doing?"

"Could ask you the same thing, doll," I clipped as I
raised a hand up to shield my eyes from the light.

"Something wrong?"

"I've locked my stupid keys in the car. I've been trying to find something to unlock the damn door, but I don't have anything," she explained exasperatedly. "I've been trying to call for stupid roadside assistance, but I can't get cell service out here in the middle of the freaking sticks."

I crossed my arms and leaned to the side, trying to get a glimpse of her face, but I couldn't see a fucking thing with that damned light shining in my eyes. Hearing that she was aggravated, I teased, "You've got a mouth on you, don't ya?"

"Yeah... well." She paused for a minute as she considered what I'd just said, then continued, "I cuss when I'm stressed. Consider it a character flaw. I'm just a little *frustrated*."

When I took a step toward her, the light from the phone dropped to her side as she staggered back, stumbling a bit before regaining her balance. "Damn it! Stupid heels," she muttered under her breath.

"Just taking a look. You alright with that?"

"Yes... please. That'd be great," she answered with a slight tremor to her voice. When I turned around and started walking towards my bike, she yelped, "Hey... wait! Where are you going? I thought you were going to help."

I didn't answer. Instead, I flipped on my bike's headlight, and then slowly turned back towards the front of the car. Once I saw the light shining directly on her, I stopped dead in my tracks. *Damn*. Just the sight of her almost knocked me off my goddamn feet. She was a stunner, but it was more than that. There was something in the way she looked at me, a vulnerability I wouldn't expect from a chick like her, and I found it hot as fuck. I took a minute to enjoy the scenery, letting my eyes drop to the pointed tip of her black high-heeled shoes, then slowly trail the length of her long, lean, sexy legs. Heat rushed through my veins as I eyed my way up to the hem of her short, gray business skirt, pausing just long enough to savor the curves of her full hips. They continued to roam over the lines of the tight-fitting black sweater that clung to her body in a way that made it impossible not to stare at her perfect breasts. When my eyes finally made their way up to her face, I couldn't help but notice the high perch of her eyebrow and the way her full lips twisted into a sexy little smirk. Damn. With just one look, she'd gotten me.

"Are you done?" she asked as she crossed her arms, drawing my attention back to her breasts.

I took a step forward and winked as I said, "I'm just getting started, doll."

Shaking her head, she stepped to the side, giving me room to see if I could get the keys out of the ignition. When I noticed that the windows were completely rolled up, I asked, "You sure you don't got a spare key hidden somewhere?"

"No," she said flatly. "My dad is always telling me that I need one, but I just haven't gotten around to it."

"No problem. How about a screwdriver?" I chuckled. "You wouldn't have one of those in that bag of yours, would ya?"

"Sorry... I think that's in my other purse," she smiled.

"Well, I left my tool bag at the house. Not going to be able to do much without it."

"Well, thanks for trying." She sighed. "I don't know what I'm going to do now."

I had a couple of options I considered offering up, most of them including me bending her over the back of her car while I was buried deep inside her, but I didn't figure she'd be the type to go for that... at least not yet, so I kept those thoughts to myself. "Looks like you got two choices, Killer. You can stay out here and pray for cell reception, or you can hitch a ride back in to town with me."

Her eyes lit up when she asked, "You mean on your motorcycle?"

"Yeah. I don't know about you, but I don't see a horse and carriage waiting for ya around the bend." I chuckled as I looked around the empty parking lot. "Everybody's gone home, and I doubt you're gonna get one of Duncan's cabs to come all the way out here."

Heat flushed across her face as she stood there staring at me with those dark, gorgeous eyes of hers. Damn. She actually liked the idea of being on the bike. I figured she'd be threatened by the Satan's Fury patch stitched on my cut and the tattoos that marked my skin.

Instead, she seemed intrigued by them. I had to admit, I liked it. I liked her. Maybe it was that sexy smile she'd given me only moments before when she caught me checking her out, or that flicker of lust in her eyes when I offered her a ride. I didn't know what it was, but at that moment, I wanted to feel her body pressed against mine, even if it was just for a ride into town.

I didn't wait for her to answer. I just got on the bike and started up the engine. When she realized I was about to leave, she grabbed her purse, quickly shoving all of her belongings back inside before she hurried back over to me. Before she got on, she asked, "You sure you don't mind?"

"Wouldn't have offered if I did," I answered as I took her purse from her and put it in the saddlebag.

With that, her hands dropped to her hips as she inched up her skirt and then threw her long, slender leg over the back of the seat like she'd done it a thousand times before. A light hint of her perfume whipped around me as she rested her delicate hands at my side, giving me an immediate sense of satisfaction.

Knowing that her sweater wouldn't be enough to protect her from the cold night air, I pulled off my cut and offered it to her as I said, "You'll want to wear this. It's gonna get cold once we start moving."

"Umm… Thanks."

She hesitantly took it from my hand. Once she put it on, my breath caught in my throat. She looked unbelievable wearing my leather. It was like the damn thing was made for her. I forced myself to stop staring and turned my focus back on the road. I started riding back towards town, trying my best to ignore the fire I felt burning deep in my gut. Her grip tightened as I pushed back the throttle and began to pick up speed, making it hard for me to decide whether I should go faster or slow down and enjoy the moment.

Having her wrapped around me was fucking with my head. Every instinct I had told me getting caught up with a girl like her would only bring a shit-ton of trouble, but I didn't give a fuck. I wanted her. Plain and simple.

Chapter 2
Marley

I never could've dreamed that my night would have taken such an interesting turn. I wasn't exactly shocked that I'd gotten lost or that I'd managed to lock the keys in my car when I stopped for dinner on the way home. Things like that just seemed to happen to me, but crossing paths with the hot biker was a surprise. When he walked up, I immediately forgot all about my stream of bad luck. He was all of my secret fantasies wrapped up in one smoking hot package. I knew he was the kind of guy my father always warned me about, but all those little pieces of advice about dangerous men on motorcycles fell on deaf ears when I stared into those beautiful blues. I couldn't help myself. I relished that feeling of intrigue swirling around in my mind when I looked at him. He was the strong and silent type, burly and rough, and absolutely the hottest guy I'd ever laid eyes on. I was lost. The man was practically towering over me with his broad shoulders and gigantic muscles rippling through his tight t-shirt, but I didn't feel threatened by him—not in the least bit. It was just the opposite. I was drawn to the captivating stranger, and it terrified me. I feared that I might lose all of my sense of reality and just throw myself at him, giving in to the lustful need that was surging through my veins. And having his jacket wrapped around me wasn't making it any easier to resist the temptation to climb him like a tree. It was bad; I was completely losing it, and the scent of his cologne mixed with leather was just about to drive me over the edge.

I had to hold it together.

I took a deep breath and stared straight ahead, trying to get a grasp on my raging libido. As we drove down that long, dark road, I couldn't help but think that I wouldn't have even met my handsome stranger if that stubborn Mr. Evan Abrams had just returned my phone call. I would've been home soaking in a nice, hot bath instead of hunting down some house in the country. But nothing ever seemed to be that easy with the people in Clallam County. I'd only been working at Smith, Wells, and Daniels Law Firm for a few months, but I already figured that some folks were just hard to deal with. As the newest associate, I was stuck managing all the cases the partners didn't want to handle, so it was no surprise that things weren't going exactly as planned with this one. There was a reason none of the others wanted to deal with the Abrams family, but it didn't matter. I had one thing on my mind: locate the son and finalize the will, period. I was determined to prove to all the men in the office that I could handle the Abrams family and whatever else they threw my way. Knowing that I couldn't afford to waste any time, I decided it was time to pay Evan Abrams a visit in person. From what I could tell, none of his family members—not even his sister—had been able to reach him, so he had no idea that his dad died a few weeks back. Since the day I was given the case, I'd been trying to sort the Abrams' family estate, and I needed to let his only son know that he and his sister had inherited the family home along with all of the land and his father's money, including his stocks and bonds. It was going to be difficult to tell a complete stranger that his father had passed away, but it had to be done. I was on my way to notify him when I got lost, which led me to locking my keys in my car at Mikey's Diner... which led me to getting on the back of *Mr. Stud Muffin's* bike. I was so screwed.

I was just starting to see the lights from town when he slowed the bike and yelled over his shoulder, "Where are we headed?"

I sighed, realizing that I was about to tell a complete stranger where I lived, but I decided to throw caution to the wind. I knew my dad was working the night shift at the precinct and my brother, Brandon, was probably sleeping. He was still trying to get over some stomach bug.

I leaned forward with my chin close to his shoulder and shouted over the loud rumble of the bike's engine, "I live on East Park Avenue. It's the blue house at the end of the street on the right. Number 601."

"Got it," he answered as he put his hand back on the accelerator, exposing several dark colored leather bracelets stacked along his wrist.

The wind caught my breath as he sped down the

long, deserted road. My body began to tremble from the chill of the night air, making me feel a tad guilty for taking his jacket. I knew he must be freezing, but I couldn't imagine how cold I would be without it. Feeling a little guilty, I leaned forward, placing my mouth close to his ear as I said, "Thanks for the ride… and for letting me wear your jacket."

"Not a problem, doll," he shouted.

I found myself wishing that the ride would last just a bit longer. I liked being on the bike with him. When we were kids, my brother would take me out riding all the time. He'd take me out on his dirt bike, exploring all the trails and woods in Cullman, Alabama, where we grew up. Eventually he managed to save enough money to buy his first motorcycle and he'd take me out from time to time, but it had been ages since I'd been out for a ride. We've both been too busy to even think about it. After we moved to Washington with our dad, we'd both gone to college and started our careers. Even though we lived in the same house, we rarely crossed paths, and I couldn't remember the last time I'd even laid eyes on my dad. Since he became the police chief, he was always busy investigating some case. No matter how small the crime, my dad treated it like a capital offense. It was just the way things were with him. He expected no less than everyone's best at all times, no excuses.

My heart started to race when he pulled onto my street. The bike's engine seemed louder than ever as we continued down the quiet street and headed for my house. I had no idea what I was so worried about. After he dropped me off, I'd never have to lay eyes on him again. I just had to get off the bike, say thank you, and get my butt in the house. Simple enough—or so I thought.

When he parked next to the curb and turned off the engine, I eased myself off of the bike and said, "Thanks again for your help. I really do appreciate it."

"Not a problem." He opened his saddlebag and reached inside for my purse. As he offered it to me, he said, "Glad I was there to help."

I took it from his hand and gave him a bashful wave as I started towards the front door. After taking a few steps, I realized that I was still wearing his jacket, so I quickly slipped it off and walked back over to him. My face blushed red as I said, "Umm… You might need this."

He hesitated for a moment, and a strange look crossing his face as he reached out and took the leather jacket from my hand. After he put it back on, he gave me a slight nod and, without another word, started his bike and drove off.

Disappointment washed over me as I watched him vanish out of sight. He hadn't asked for my number. He hadn't even asked for my name. He just took off like he was relieved to be rid of me, and I hated that it bothered me so much. I couldn't shake the regret that was building in the back of my mind. I wanted to know more about the enigmatic stranger, and the part that got to me the most was that I wanted him to *want* to know more about me as well. Yep, I was off my rocker.

Berating myself all the way to the front door, I stepped inside and found my brother lying on the sofa with a cold rag on his head. He looked like death warmed over, so I tried not to get too close as I asked, "Hey, bro. You feeling any better?"

"I'm fine," he grumbled. Even though he was two years older than me, owned his own construction company, and could take on a pack of wolves with his bare hands, the man acted like a big ol' whiny baby whenever he was sick. On days like this, he was just downright pitiful. So I did my best to avoid him at all costs when he wasn't feeling well.

"Okay, then. You sure you don't need anything?"

"Nah," he murmured with his eyes closed. "I'm fine."

As I headed for the stairs, I said, "Okay, suit yourself. I'm headed to bed."

I'd just hit the first step when he asked, "You gonna tell me who that was?"

"Who?" I knew exactly who he was talking about.

"The guy on the 2015 Limited Edition Harley Road Glide Special that just pulled up to our house and dropped you off?"

"Oh... umm... I don't know. Just some guy. I had a little car trouble, so he offered to bring me home," I explained.

"Why didn't you call me?"

Big

Knowing he'd crawl all over me for locking my keys in the car, I lied, "I knew you weren't feeling well, so I just—"

He yanked the rag off of his forehead and sat up on the sofa. He reminded me of our father as he glared at me with his dark brown eyes and bellowed, "Dammit, Marley Jo. Who knows who this guy is? He could've–"

Before he could continue, I held up my hand and shouted, "Don't even start with me, Brandon. I managed to survive just fine, and I don't need a lecture from you... or Dad."

"You got lucky this time." He coughed and grumbled as he fell back on his pillow and placed the rag back on his forehead. "Where'd you leave your car? I'll go take a look at it in the morning."

I knew he'd ask. He always asked. It was one of the many negatives of living in the same house with two overbearing men. When Mom died, I had thought moving in with my dad was the best way to help him. I needed a place to stay; I'd just graduated from law school and started my job at the firm in town. It just made sense. Then, Brandon had decided to build a house and moved in with Dad when construction began. It was good to be all together again, but now the house seemed so much smaller than it did when we were kids. All sense of privacy was gone. If Brandon found out I didn't have my keys, he'd have a cow. So I did the only thing I knew to do: I lied.

I walked over to the front door and locked the

deadbolt as I said, "I've already called a wrecker service. I knew you weren't feeling good, so I just told them to go out there and get it."

"Why'd you go and do that? Do you have any idea how expensive that is?"

"I do… and I said I took care of it," I told him as I turned and stormed up the stairs, avoiding any chance that he'd tell me to cancel the tow. Once I was in my room, I quickly threw on my pajamas and curled into bed. I was exhausted, but there was no way I was going to get any sleep. I couldn't stop thinking about him—the sexy curve of his lips when he smiled, the intoxicating scent of his cologne, the spark in his eyes when he looked at me, and the way my body tingled when I got on his bike and wrapped my arms around him. Every breath I took brought on another thought or memory, and there was nothing I could do to stop it, and I wasn't so sure I wanted to. I liked the way I felt when I was with him.

I stared at the ceiling for hours, reliving every moment I'd shared with him, and the longer I lay in the bed, the harder it was to stay there. I decided to stop fighting it and got up. I put on my bathrobe and once I had my slippers on, I headed downstairs to the kitchen for a cup of coffee. It was early, long before my dad or brother would be getting up, so I decided to take advantage of the quiet. While my coffee was brewing, I headed out to the front door to get the morning paper. As usual, it just barely made it to the porch and was teetering on the side of the deck. I picked it up and was just about to step back inside when I noticed my car pulling into the driveway. I stood there and watched as it stopped right at the garage door. The door opened, and a tall, muscular man with a baseball cap and cowboy boots, looking like he'd been plucked right out of a cotton field in Tennessee, stepped out of the car. I was a little taken aback to see Farmer John walking towards me.

As he reached the front steps, he smiled and said, "We got your car for ya."

"We?" I cocked my head to the side and studied him for a moment before I asked, "Umm… and who are you?"

"Oh… I'm sorry, ma'am. I'm Boozer. One of the brothers from the club. Smokey wanted me to get your car back to you before you had to go to work, so…" he told me as he extended his hand out to me. I could only assume that the Smokey he was referring to was the biker guy from last night. I thought back to those gorgeous, blue eyes and that black beard and wondered how he'd managed to get the nickname Smokey. I was lost in my thoughts when Boozer continued, "Here ya go."

I took the keys from him. "Thank you… umm, *Boozer*. I really appreciate it. How much do I owe you?"

"Not a thing, Sweet Pea. Smokey took care of it." Then he started walking towards the road. Just as he reached the sidewalk, a black SUV pulled up next to him. Before he got in the truck, he waved at me and shouted, "Let us know if you need anything else."

Before I could stop him, he slammed his door. Goosebumps began to prickle against my skin as the truck inched away from the curb. Feeling a strange sensation that I was being watched, I pulled my robe tighter around my waist and stared at the dark-tinted windows, trying to see if I could make out who was sitting in the driver's seat. Warmth rushed over me when I noticed a familiar dark beard and a wrist covered in the same leather bracelets I'd seen last night.

It was him. I couldn't stop myself from watching the SUV as it slowly made its way down the street, and I suddenly became scared that it might be the last time I'd ever see my mysterious biker.

Did you enjoy this excerpt?
Look for "Smokey" available on Amazon.com!

Made in the USA
San Bernardino, CA
01 August 2017